Ghosts of Icarus

NIGEL PEARCE

I0665390

CHIPMUNKA CLASSICS

CHIPMUNKA CLASSICS

Published by
Chipmunkapublishing
United Kingdom

http://www. chipmunkaclassics.co.uk

Copyright © Nigel Pearce 2015

ISBN   978-1-78382-226-3

Supported using public funding by

**ARTS COUNCIL
ENGLAND**

LOTTERY FUNDED

The Ghosts of Icarus

The ghosts of Icarus are howling their haunting,
Rise like Lady Lazarus before the moon is bright,
Spectres delight in demanding a dreamy delirium,
They dance like rising dead, burrowing up eagerly
From their bejewelled tombs, my casket is cracked.

A doctor looks away in shame; he is not to blame,
The foe we fought cannot be bought by him or us,
We are the patients, addicts and prisoners in chains,
Bound, tight, chocking this entombment crushes me,
For the ghosts of Icarus are bellowing within a brain.

Death's wings open to embrace my mother in the fields of moonshine

Night closed her arms around your soul in a dance of stars,

That universe of vibrations is where my eyes sting with love,

You gave me the literature of dreams; there we learnt to hide,

We were stretched between the poles of our flows and ebbing.

Our hymn, a wilderness of fated roaming in search of crystal,

Wandering with tears that burnt those pleas touching colours,

An effusion of whispers surrounded by the drama of outsiders,

We walked through corn fields which were like a golden veil.

Rocked you to sleep, verse vibrating around a sea of lunar light,

Time has wrapped you in a melody, the meander of dreaminess.

Zero

I am
Not an ice cube to be thawed with therapy, E.C.T,
In my core poetry and love burns melted the tears,
They are weeping in that solitude where hail storms,
The frost-bite consumes, it has devoured my heart.

When I introspect into many souls all I see is a zero,
Just the dilated pupils of their eyes and wastelands,
They see don't see anything when look a a solitary.

Mrs. W

Most human beings have just two eyes blinking,
Bertolt Brecht said: 'the Party has a thousand.'
Mrs. W had a Third Eye, the Eye of a Buddha,
She spotted me hiding within lines of words,
Read my literature, saw something sparkle,
Gave Thomas, Lawrence, Camus, this feast,
I bloomed, petals opened to expose a writer,
Was out of place and time the school was not,
Sought nourishment in a wilderness of nettles.

"He is a rose who left in this desert will wilt", she
Warned and within a year *acid* melted my mind.

P.B.

So 'cool' people thought, a Marxist philosophy lecturer,
Ideal foster father with his counterbalance the Catholic,
You know they only visited me once in hospital, absent
Twenty-five years as fashions for some people change.

He left The Party, apparently a question of theoretical
Schism, I knew him a little better, had read his poems,
Everything an abstract challenge, dialectics in his head,
Poetry can give a glimpse of the person behind the
walls.

The rub was he was still in love with a woman in the
stars,
He left the organization; he had risked prison for the
Party.

S.B.

They called you the Acid Queen at fifteen,
The best 'fuck' in town amongst teenage
Aphrodites, but we would commune mind
Tuned into mind and yes, you wrote as well,
I was two years younger, rebellion red rebel,
Tripped out, you saw my vein haemorrhage,
You claimed it was that stopped you fixing.

Foetus cast out of a womb you grew so strange,
I don't think you slept with the men you liked but
Those who were an equivalent to a line of speed,
You did LOVE, but was always your sunrise too
Soon evening and night, there was Sue and me.

The Party provided a fine funeral too early for me.

Dr. E.I.

Bluestocking, blue steel, iron in the soul,
You put me in a locked adult ward at 14,
Back to adolescent unit merry-go-round,
Round and round adult wards correction,
One day you smiled I thought it was okay,
Most favoured lady, the disturbed teenager,
You explained the dark arts of your trade,
Two years in Hollymoor Hospital my home.

You crafted a book; it was the standard text,
The unit was renamed the Irwin Unit, I'd left,
I perused those lines of spite and contempt,
You must have hated some of us in reality,
The tears of blood run down burnt cheeks.

G.C.

An enigma in stagnation, embalmed,
A leaf that fell from the tree of death,
Were mute, was it all that Stelazine?
Or you'd gone to paradise or Hades.

Just vanished one day, media alert,
Wandered off, seized, no one knew,
They even dredged a local reservoir,
Not a puzzle solved, never forgotten.

Professor T.

You had a brand new toy, the experimental unit,
You took interesting patients to examine carefully,
Manic-depression was your 'thing', all types done,
I absconded, injection when the police returned me.

Slowed, slower and slow down a dust pipe I went,
Lost interest in the hospital food, the Bread of Life,
On bed-rest twenty-four hour watch, this is torment,
You enforce my order, enforced E.C.T, wired me up.

Hurray, a cured patient to display to medical students,
We sat, their pens posed, I talked about Totskyism,
They scribbled, you smiled and said'back to the ward'.

'Worse things happen at sea.' he would say.

H...
H is for Hell,
H is for Heroin,
H is for Heaven,
H is for Helpless,
H is for Hopeless,
H is for Homeless,

Should have been aborted and
Lived in the safety of a bell jar.

S is for Schizophrenia,
S is for Solitude,
S is for Suicide.

Fled fragrant suffocation in Eden
For the bitter taste of brown sugar,
A star shone and clasped my mind,
A morning was star-fixed to score.

.

M.A.

A wolf in hippie clothing, no less a lamb for that,
A wizard in nappies, with those blunted needles,
Those syringes that would get stuck in the rush,
'Cool man, got any gear, any beer, anything at all.'
Those brews we would cook, crushed 'blues' plus,
Speed with barbiturates, speed with speed, speed.

The rest of your fear and loathing, my pen runs dry.

S.

You were not 'scum' in the circle,
You could always find the mainline,
Wondered about the tattoo swastika,
No, not a neo-Nazi, but a Hell's Angel.

I heard you lost a leg, bad hit gangrene,
You seemed so gentle, a sheep in wolf's...

Dr. C (psychiatrist).

The Brain without the gears required to be
A consultant psychiatrist, one of the best
Minds have met, worked in parallel lines,
He has me on a gram of Chlorpromazine,
He says R.D. Laing is 'profoundly disturbed',
I say 'Thank you for crucifying me with meds.'
I say: 'Are you always so calm', human voice:
'Even when I am very angry Nigel', I wonder?

Dr. C (psychologist).

Behind those silk scarves, smiles and sophistication,
There was a mind as reductionist as your husband's,
Biochemistry, bio-chemistry alone, you teach coping,
To cope with the symptoms of chemical malfunction,
I don't think you ever really believed it black and white.

Your edifice came tumbling around you, I wept
Largactil,
Perhaps you now see train lines meet and derail a train.

A.M

Blond goddess of the underground, of the revolution,
My back would be crisscrossed, your ecstasy scratches,
Our first year crashed into that second was Year Zero,
Would-be urban guerrilla you sold out the Struggle and
I,
A very nice lectureship with all the trimmings, how do
you
Square the circle perhaps you were always running
giddy.

Love and revolution, art and poetry you and I
became…
So lost and bewildered with without 'love in the
struggle.'

'Goodbye 'I said, 'love is not enough' she replied, a
catch.

L.M.

Dawn's death hung like a first kiss,
Dawn, she wore a wondrous shroud,
Woven from the honey of dew scent,
And her eyes echoed Time's echoing,
Like the chimes of a pendulum swaying.

She weaved a veil which obscured eyes,
Like November mist brushes countryside,
And spinning her thread from the Alpha,
She worked to the pulse of his red Earth.

For who with her senses unbounded
Could awake at Dawn's deathly delight,
Or ignore the timing a spinning wheel,
Forget stroking shimmer of summer day.

But the thread she wove was awful, mortal,
Was this leaden Earthly sphere, she knew.

You were third time lucky, we buried you

In Praise of Katherine Mansfield.[1]

All of those bourgeois women thought you were merely

A writer of cream tea fancies,

Something to be eaten and discussed in polite company,

To read without dark discord,

That is how your minimizer, a hated one who maimed words,

Your husband contrived a legacy, he would have succeeded,

 But pristine manuscripts hoarded from the foe,

Your death had confounded all but the sisters of Antigone,

Bees who kept the wax,

Your honey was tainted by dark mind puerile man,

Not beloved of words,' bees hum

Bees sang manuscripts back

No censorious cancerous chocolate box sweetness.

Your stories were not howlers of slogans or

Phallic thrusts like many in time of hope and hate,

Weeper of words about woes of the world's women and the outcasts

Lesbian love, moonlight and the Aloe,

The white child runs away with aboriginals,

The police caught the child, thought-police tried to catch you,

---

[1] it became clear as a result of feminist scholarship that the short-stories of Mansfield as published by her
  Husband did not reflect the full depth and 'double discourse' that Katherine had intended.

Love lightens corruption and your cry was one of
'Bliss'[2]

An ascent into the heavens where writers are in love
with words

---

[2] 'Bliss' (1918) was one of Katherine Mansfield's most
notable short-stories.

A poet taking the advice of Timothy Leary: *'turn on, tune in, drop out'* **or how to become an acid casualty.**

A large white skull is blown smooth and shiny by sand,

the

DATE

is

1973

the

SKULL

has

BECOME

an

ALABASTER TEMPLE

in which priestesses of Venus prepare the magic host,

Lysergic acid diethamide,

the sacrament of poetry

it must be kept quite cool; it was cool, diving into lime

green oceans of the unconscious, finding self in embryo,

soaring on currents of the mind's air way above steeples,

peaking too metamorphose into a moment of orange breath.

Then came a sickness, it just eats away the mind, it becomes

impossible to close the door of the unconscious once opened.

'a lost letter'.

A lost letter was crumbled; your brown hair was always nice and scruffy, you had an aversion to cold water because of the spots. In the 'Settlement' people tried to make sense of thunder storms, but the lightning hurt our eyes. Why is the wall dissolving into mist? Rainer I'm sure that East Germany was never really the 'Socialist Motherland', our pint glasses stood empty. We all lived in this commune; there we talked of psychology and revolution and had nervous breakdowns. Ed was obsessed by the poetry of Leonard Cohen, but his walls were stroked by his own poems. A large shiny steel toaster sat surrounded by white and brown breadcrumbs, it took four slices at one go. We were stoned and laughing uncontrollably, tried to stop the giggles but they tore through the paper silence, then, my God, arrived our social worker, we must stop this hysteria and eat our toast and marmite in an orderly fashion.

'I'm sorry Dr. Irwin, I've let you down'.

'No Francis, the only person you have let down is yourself'.

'Yes mother'. I think to myself.

A chalky yellow tablet, a large white one shaped like a flying saucer and a tiny blue one are placed in my hand, take them like a communicant receiving the Host at Mass. I'm glad of the oblivion because it's like the touch of autumn, chill and golden. I'm discharged, and then dive into a pool of purple light to swim with shoals of orange fish.

Sonnet for my other lost family.

They did mistake a tear with their Idea,
The bat it flies, no eyes, no illusion,
You came beyond their world without that fear,
A sound of sand at dusk, not pollution;
The heat just roared until the brain it boils,
But was a transmitter for Lukács,
They had then reaped the gains and spoils,
Your brain had rays which had already a stash;
You were the type to make them look a twit,
When the epoch did not collapse a clown,
You moved into business, they like a twit,
The tide had turned and you had not a frown.
The group would soon just use your name,
    I thought it more than just a shame

Venus.

A
serpent
of mauve eases

into
her temple, the
muscles tighten

but
like particles
of grit in parched

eyes
that sting
and throb, she

sobs
in silence,
for his pen only

writes
only in the
language of phosphorus,

they
burn into each
other with a blaze

of
forgetfulness
until sucked dry

they lie with limbs limp like leaves that are blown into
tomorrow.

Lines on William Burroughs' concept of 'death-in-life'.

Square
hearts had
stopped, they were

Just
rusty bilge
pumps, someone turned

The
switch off,
what a turn-on

Never
dug that
scene with America

And
atom bombs,
chant with those

Of
us who
have a different

                        sound

                                and

                                            song
to the hooded-snake death dirge, breath an autumn
                                         wind
                                of

pure

        purgation,

howl

        cathartic

baby   burnout

buzz   madness.

He had placed

enigma in caps.

opened that cap, cooked it,

                     fixed

it, again, again, hazy.

DECONDITIONED HIMSELF FROM STATE
SUBLIMNIAL MIND MANIPULATION,
He had the sweet-death golden flight of Icarus, also the
endless labour of Sisyphus.

Unlike Burroughs I did get clean, but the purple lights
they did remain floating free.

The beauty of vultures.

The vulture circles solitary,
He has the beauty of outcasts
Soaring over the wastelands,

His hooked beak tears the stones,
It is a ritual of cleansing carrion,
They smile with jets of icy blood.

Laboratory Experiment Revisited

Red tentacles are gripping the wasted wail of a seething
brain

which writhes in delirium with $C_{10}H_{15}N$ rush,
white light;

Eyes hang loose attached only by yellow threads to grey
sockets,

They melted a millisecond ago and now are dripping,
dropping

by diamond drop into a culture dish, the doctor makes
a smear,

Places a slide beneath the lens of a microscope and
peers in, a

child yells into her eyes, she jumps back too late as the
laboratory

rotates into concentric circles, it has become a
phantasmagoria,

The pain had gone, but so had a memory of a brain
that is sane.

Note: $C_{10}H_{15}N$ is the formula for
methamphetamine (Methedrine).

Butterflies lead the struggle against the neo-fascists and their lackeys.

A
fragile butterfly
is spiked on a rusty pin
of twisting hatred, that is stabbing

Like
a hot poker, the
fascist knifes shred his mind
and carve their emblems into innocent

Folds
of flesh, their storm
is grinning a lightening of glares,
those eyes are squirming like shoals

Of
fish swimming into this room,
the faces of fascists are mutating
until only the façade of brick remains,

Their
scowls are mono-zero,
a dark harvest only reaped
by the moralists of work and the book burners,

Fire begins to flare fromthe wings of the butterflies, it
forms into flames and shapes the word "resistance".

Song to the oppressed: "never trust men in suits".

A howl encrusted with sores and dressed in the persuasive vestments of

An abomination slips from those contracting grins, that is the priest enrobed

In the cloak of an abortionist greets the pleated wail of another cocktail Party,

Another nightmare, so let them cruise in their seas of dollars and moral excrement,

Beware you anachronisms because lava of the oppressed is beginning to bubble,

We say: "No shit you pigs, we're going to sweep away the dust from your theatre",

You entombed bourgeois whose ballet of cardboard replicas is step, step, stepping

To the tolling of a Death Bell, it is beginnings to ring in their ears and they wince with

Fear, our hammer, the mallet of History is striking their sculls only to reveal vacuum.

The writing of verse by night.

The poet of the night's desert begins to scribble like
the waves into an ocean whose mist is without dawn,

Drifting across these fields with wonder, like the touch
into swaying seas of corn and sun, sigh with the lovers

Like the oceans, their caress is dripping like wax and
breath
onto paper flowers, swirling into an endless spiral of
clouds.

Moonshine weeps into this ocean of nothingness, the
dust
is like a masquerade which is dissolving into white and
zero,

The masks melt softening into visions like their opiate
oblivion
With eyes the shining, shadows like an insomnia of
dreaming.

Spring's dancers wander across the virgin page with its
sighing,
this is a word beginning to form into a wave, a whisper
of sand,

The cloaked pen weaves into this morning shimmer of
cobwebs
in which the Muse hangs suspended like eternity
cloaked in ivy.,
A poet must catch a Muse and devour it with the
delight of God.

'Vade retro Satana.' #2

You are a player of games so transparent it is so
questionable if are a Grandmaster,

Maybe it is true to claim Sirius as a birthplace, but you
certainly are no Stockhausen,

I know you have pushed several people over a
precipice just for a thwarted ambition,

Some others are roused as you have defiled a dead man
a suicide, he was the artist.

The first suicide whose friends you still call 'scum' was
just one Lumpenproletarian,

You're fairly Lumpen yourself a cancerous lump we
may cut out before it claws out,

Your kneecaps may benefit from a swift clean surgical
cut you need an anaesthetic,

That incessant oozing of poison to people about
Broadmoor lunacy, just so boring.

We protect the masses before your mechanical fame
wood knurled mind yells loud,

Like all of your type you are no more than a token
reproduction, an entire derivative,

Our artist, his portraits were imprudent, but no need to
accuse him of that sort of rap,

Throwing that kind of filth at him while riding your
glorious white charger is just crap.

A presentiment of your destiny in its own living hell, so
don't keep conjuring it all up,

We may be compelled to exorcise, no *Vade retro Satana,*
but a self-mirrored image.

The moon falling into morning.

The

       moon

           has

               fallen

                    like

freedom

in a

frenzied

                   hum

             until

        her

     bonds

unravel

 as

 she

     moans

         the

            sighing

                into

morning.

A Beam Of Hope This Year

A death pyre fire was the light that had dominated two
thousand and fourteen,

The stench of my burning flesh accompanied each
essay, every poem written,

I was intoxicated and revolted by the odours of my
post-addiction death,

Thirty years clean and dry, degrees acquired poetry and
prose published it is cruel.

A new treatment and the consultant has agreed,

It is like the rising sun fondling

And stroking what had been the darkest of nights, not
the dark night of the soul,

No, it would have been the oblivion of the tomb; not a
belief in resurrection here.

Together with medics and the medicines a new dawn a
birth in life may well be.

A Beam Of Hope This Year (Revised)

A death pyre fire was the fire which had burned
throughout two thousand and fourteen,

The stench of my burning flesh accompanied each
breath and essay any poem scribed,

I was intoxicated and revolted by the odours of my
post-addiction, this a dance of death

Thirty years clean and dry, degrees, poetry and prose
published it seems damned cruel.

A new treatment and the consultant has agreed, it was
like the rising sun aglow fondling

And stroking what had been the darkest of night, this
was not the Dark Night of the Soul,

No, it would have been the oblivion of the tomb; fir
there not a belief in resurrection here.

Together with medics and the medicines a new dawn a
birth in life may well have become.

Stars are cast in cruel constellation a curse is cast as the
cost is the medicine is so high.

THE POEMS OF A SHEPHERD UPON WAKING ONE FROSTY MORNING.

Poem # 1. Sonnet 18 revisited: [A Shakespearean Sonnet.]

Should I compare you to a frame of steel?
My sheep just know the wind is confusion,
At Mass they fear to feast upon that meal,
We dry a sea of tears with illusion.
The hum of minds is such a bloody bolt,
He was a wire of fire, a ghostly Lukács,
One school of thought always was bought,
He had radar that zoomed into the cash.
Your type is not for us because of misfit,
The night is still the banks the painted clown,
Forgot and went into dollars, you twit,
The tide had turned; you did not cast a frown.

    The God who read these finite lines,
      I have a fear of Him; I know the signs.

Poem # 2 The Shepherdess: [A Villanelle].

We thawed a frosty reality to dissolve ice with love,
time it will tell,

Our eyes, whose moistened pupils could swallow their
hardened gaze,

She soared across the tempestuous Cosmos, a star of
dust it can swell.

We crucified any betrayal of damned love, refused the
death knell,

That dark spark, we conceived this just like evaporating
into a haze,

We thawed a frosty reality to dissolve ice with love,
time it will tell.

I touched with delicate fingers the clasp on your eyes,
they had a spell,

A stream with the purple fragrance of humming, a
goddess was ablaze,

She soared across the tempestuous Cosmos; a star of
dust it can swell.

You crumpled into a sphere of sighs, of white light, a
dove in hell,

Whose wings were cursed as we dived into the sun in
joyful daze?

We thawed a frosty reality to dissolve ice with love,
time it will tell.

Our song was vibrating into the tree which was
weeping nectar's jell,

Sipped each other's ancient milk, a sacred libation of
pristine praise,

She soared across the tempestuous Cosmos; a star of dust it can swell.

Tangerine it intertwines in a frenzy of breath, struck a golden bell,

Then we lay exhausted in a grave, our bodies consumed and fazed,

We thawed a frosty reality to dissolve ice with love, time it will tell,

She soared across the tempestuous Cosmos, a star of dust it can swell

Poem #3. The Shepherd contemplates writing upon waking: [A Pantoum].

I woke with a web of words upon my face,
The night left a stain and taste of almond,
I wonder what this may mean; it was lace,
The taste was as bitter as a Norse legend.

The night left a stain and taste of almond,
She had sucked a word, the womb denied,
The taste was as bitter as a Norse legend,
They had come into my mind like cyanide

She had sucked a word, the womb denied,
The birth pangs were like a tomb that lied,
They had come into my mind like cyanide,
I wrote with the holy writ and then I died.

The birth pangs were like a tomb that lied,
She smiled and I knew this was true grace,
I wrote with the holy writ and then I died,
I woke with a web of words upon my face.

**Poem #4 The shepherd ponders the Steppenwolf.
(A Petrarchan Sonnet.)**

I write the Golden Mean of eight to five,
My job to keep my sheep in an order,
The sheep would rue a marauder,
My crook the pen by which I live,
The game is not to work between 8 and 5,
Those hours must keep the sheep inside,
A mist descends; it masks the bold boulder,
The stone is rolled by wolfish stockholder,
It shall not hit my sheep whom I drive to thrive.

The grey wolf roams across the steppe,
Alone yet proud he is the one they fear,
For wolves must eat the meat of sheep,
He wanders without a single misstep,
He has a coat of fur quite grey like Lear,
Although alert and quick, a slick sidestep.

Poem #5 The Shepherd remembers the Greek partisans. [A villanelle].

The dawn awakes; it is cloaked in snow;
This melts to leave a bare, a bleak terrain,
My cloak is of red unlike the black crow.

This morning I know a knife will glow,
I shall shake with shame, with the stain,
The sheep to the slaughter must go below.

They do not know that irresistible flow
of seasonal cruelty, a brute the agrarian,
My cloak is of red unlike the black crow.

A vocation of pain the shepherds know,
Must herd innocents to the subterranean,
The sheep to the slaughter must go below.

No, not bow to that ancient status quo,
An act of revolt, he had been a partisan,
The dawn awakes, it is cloaked in snow.

In Greek hills blood must always flow,
Sappho the struggle of Syriza must pen,
My cloak is red unlike the black crow,
The sheep to the slaughter must go below.

Some Rambling on the Shepherd Cycle

I note a contradiction commented on by Marx (Marx (2007), p.394) in *Grundrisse* that there is no direct connection between a society's material development and the artistic flourishing of that society. I use this to contextualize my commentary. The cycle of poetry began with an idea about *Pastoral* with an awareness that the **term** like the sonnet is derived from the Renaissance and the Italian countryside for *pastor* translates into shepherd. However the **genre** suited my purposes and can be found to emanate from *Idylls* of Theocritus (c. 310-250 BC.) which is considered to be the origins of ancient Greek bucolic poetry. Greece was at the forefront of my mind because of the recent victory of Syriza and the hopes for a more 'just' society. Like Elizabeth Bishop, whose work is examined in (Neale (2009, Ch.15) especially in the context of 'the freedom of form' I also found with 'forms':

They seem to start the machinery going.

Neale (2009) p. 246.

For my first sonnet title I took the advice of Neale 2009. p240) and 'tested the sonnet' referencing both Shakespeare's *Sonnet 18* and Bob Dylan *Highway 61 Revisited*, hence *Sonnet 18 Revisited*. During the composition of this sonnet I was aware of what Dan Paterson (1999) calls the:

…. The dialectical scheme of thesis, antithesis and synthesis. And er, a bit left over.

Paterson (1999) p. xxii

Of course 'the bit left over' is the couplet, which after the thesis of the first quatrain, its antithesis in the second and the synthesis with the final quatrain, represents the 'Volta' or dialectical leap. Mine is consistent with the sonnet as a form of love poetry, but this one is about a betrayal of a belief system by a respected and cared for person.

The cycle continues with a villanelle about the shepherd's love for a shepherdess, I am staying attached to the *Pastoral* of a shepherd in an idyll of a kind. I use a 'long-line' rather like Walt Whitman rather than the shorter beats of a traditional villanelle to attempt to capture the sense of motion and flight. However, it does, I think, work as a villanelle and maintains the rhyme and refrain scheme:

abA1, abA2, abA1, abA2, abA1, aaA1A2.

The Pantoum is quite orthodox. The first and therefore last lines came upon me just like a phantom upon waking and required no editing:

'I woke with a web of words upon my face,'

In *Poem #4 A Shepherd ponders the Steppenwolf* illustrates a lifelong admiration for Hermann Hesse's novel *Steppenwolf* in the Sestet and marks the Volta with the Octave which plays with Paterson's concept (1999 p. xvii-xxii) that the predominance of a Volta on or slightly after the 8th line can be attributed to our biological predetermination to the 'Golden Mean' or Fibonacci sequence the ratio of 8.5 so you would have 13 lines. But couldn't because Judas was the thirteenth disciple and so the sonnet must be fourteen lines. This Paterson claims as a theory of the neurological and cultural origin of the Petrarchan sonnet. Poem #5 draws the threads together and creates some links between Arcadia and modernity. It employs enjambment. The conflict within modern Greece referencing the Communist Party partisans who drove out the Nazis only to be vanquished by the British and American military. Also the current tensions on the Left are explored with the 'black crow' metaphor for Anarchist/Autonomists who have attacked both Marxists and the State Apparatus. We discover that the shepherd has a relation to Sappho, perhaps, is a reincarnation of the poet? Finally, I did find 'the freedom of form liberating', but would also like to place it in relation to the nature of poetry generally as encapsulated by the 1971 Noble Prize Literature winner Pablo Neruda who writes persuasively:

Before the printing press poetry flourished. That is why we know poetry is like bread; should be shared by all, scholars and by peasants, by our vast, incredible, extraordinary family of humanity.'

- Neruda (2014) p 1.

Bibliography

Leonard, J (2005) *The Poetry Handbook*, Oxford: Oxford University Press.

Leonard, J (2013) *Oxford Rhyming Dictionary*, Oxford: Oxford University Press.

Marx, K (2007) (ed) McLellan. *Selected Writings*, Oxford, Oxford University Press.

Neale, D. (ed.) (2009) *A Creative Writing Handbook*, Milton Keynes/London: A & C Black in association with The Open University.

Neruda, P (2014) (ed) Eisner. *The Essential Neruda*, Northumberland: Blood Axe Books.

Paterson, D (ed) (1999) *101 Sonnets*, London: Faber & Faber.

Williams, R (2013) *The Poetry Toolkit*, London: Bloomsbury.

'The Social Workers will come and take you away.'
(A short-story)

'The social workers will come and take you away if you write about what goes on at home with your stories that you always seem to be writing at school' my mother said.

I did not reply, what could an eight year old child say in what his older sister referred to as the 'Fear pit.' All I knew that I tried to spend every moment at school I could, but the school did not provide any real sanctuary. There were Fiona and Graham, two older children who had guessed things were not quite right and sought to protect me from the other children who kept chanting:

'Nutty Nigel, Nutty Nigel'

Or if I did make an attempt to explain, the taunts would change:

'Jackanory, Jackanory' the name of a children's story programme at the time.

The other children went to parties, birthday parties and suchlike. No one was allowed to enter Dungeon Pearce, they might get an inkling. On one occasion Peter's mother invited me to his birthday party, I was given a copy of 'Adventure Stories for Boys' and told to be careful about my language. When I entered this palace of delights I could not play with the other children, I didn't know how. To my astonishment pop music was played, it was banned at the 'fear pit', although my sister had smuggled in some Donovan and Rolling Stones which were quickly discovered and banished. They began to dance, it was like another world, they danced as they pleased, to express themselves with their bodies, and I stood embarrassed at the very edge of the room. Simply didn't know what to do, but I noticed Sharon, who danced to the music of Lulu like a priestess of Dionysus.

When I first attended school at the age of five, it had just been mum and I. My sister was away at Public 'pep' school and father was away at work or at sea in a bottle of whisky. To my utter astonishment the boys chased a bag of wind round a field, it seemed absurd to me. Soon I would be reading about Zoology and then History.

Home was Hell.

I saw my mother and father involved in physical fights, J' used to duck the blows though, too agile for a middle-aged ex-soldier. The first time she ran away, they found her 'sleeping rough' on Brighton beach.

My allegiances were beginning to change.

Mother had made her a set of really boring clothes when she was brought back. Not for J' though, a psychedelic mini of mini dresses appeared. She wasn't going to be cowered and was now mixing with the hippies in Notting Hill, unknown to my parents.

It was the Mater who first guessed what was going down. Much to my astonishment and abhorrence she would, after my sister left for school, but before I did 'steam open 'J's mail and read selected passages out aloud:

'…

That is disgusting.

…

'Filthy.'

They were just a teenage girl's love letters.

However, she was starting to let her appearance slip; she stopped washing and did smell rather strong. The Patriarch confronted her with shouts and fists. A social worker Miss Mac… was assigned to my sister and sussed out that the family was indeed a 'fear pit', but he rang social services and accused the woman of making lesbian advances to my sister: nonsense. She was taken off the case and within days my sister had run away again, this time to a hippy commune.

In the late 60's every Christmas the 'plain clothes' police did a 'sweep' of Soho, Gerrard Street, etc. eyes peeled for missing hippies. My sister would have been 16 on Boxing Day and free. They caught her at 15 and she was 'carrying' on Christmas Eve. Over Christmas she stayed in a Remand Centre, they sentenced her to be detained until age 18 at a specialist unit for emotionally disturbed girls. Within six months of her discharge, she would be married and admitted to the Maudsley psychiatric hospital.

They wanted to perform a leucotomy, but she went into therapy.

The social workers would take me away a few years later…

My sister and I would become estranged years later. As she said:

'I can fool any doctor, but I can't fool you.'

The only person she really fooled was herself.

Years later when I became aware Why Elise?

Why write about Elise Cowen? It is rhetorical; a Beat poet, they were the precursors to the counter-culture, obsessed with books, rejected her roots, depressive becoming psychotic, spent time in psychiatric hospital, and had hepatitis as a result of her drug use. She was different from many of her contemporaries and found it difficult to play the roles her generation attempted to impose on her; for this she would pay a high price, a premature death. Elise jumped through a closed seventh floor window to her death at the age of 29. Why did she crucify herself with hypodermic needles? I am 55 and may know, also having drug-related schizophrenia, a writer, but I have been 'clean' and 'dry' for over thirty years.

Since 2014 the conditions for a revaluation of her poetry existed with the publication of Elise Cowen's only complete notebook ['Fall 1959-Spring 1960'] Trigilio (2014) and of her life with the republication of Elise's friend's Joyce Johnston (2014*) Come and Join the Dance* in which Elise is Kay. This is in addition to her other primary source Johnston (2006) *Minor Characters: a brief memoir of the Beat Generation* and Skir (1970) *Every Green Review, October 1970* both provide a wealth of material. The whole process of revealing this 'hidden history' of women 'Beat' writers could be traced to Neil Cassady's [the Muse of Allen Ginsberg and Jack Kerouac] partner Carolyn Cassady, who came out about the 'Beat' men in Cassady (1990) *Off The Road: Twenty Years with Cassady, Kerouac and Ginsberg*. Her book was a sharp rebuke to the men of the Beat Generation. It was of course a pun on Jack Kerouac (2000) *On the Road* written in 1957 which was the cornerstone of male Beat fiction with Allen Ginsberg, he was intimately involved with Elise Cowen for a brief period, who's *Howl* (2014) was published, after an obscenity trial, in 1956 and provided the poetic foundation. I cast a shadow on the Beat's personal revolution as it did not produce a qualitative social transformation, a socialist revolution, only a quantitative shift in social values. Elise and I were writing as well.

The Hit.

'Go man go.'   Elise encourages.

As every junky knows there was a family dysfunction or three: Blessed Trinity. However, it is cast into Hades because Elise like I remembered that first hit of heroin. She said:

What America needs is a lot of cheap heroin.

Skir (1970) p10.

Aged twelve, my mind was unlocked by L.S.D facilitating the comprehension of poetry: 'The force that through the green fuse drives the flower' (Thomas 1972, p. 8). Aged thirteen, I mixed with students like Elise, also an avid reader of Dylan Thomas (Skir 1970, p. 3). We sought sanctuary in a company of souls who did not yell, new companions did not have the strut of oppression and welcomed all outsiders into the company of dreamers, and these people were not branded with the iron of hypocrisy. They caressed with potions, wondrous white powders which beckoned into worlds of meaning and caring. Initiating a world of compassion and the poetry of oblivion, they prepared our first fix. The pristine white powder floated into a spoon, a lighter ignites, a wait until the liquid began to bubble with significance, cotton wool put in place with the zeal of the mystic in the magic liquid, the glass syringe sighed as the plunger is drawn up. Hell would cease now and the heavens danced to caress the verse in the mind of the poets. Those shackles floated away, the needle fitted snugly onto the syringe, the singer of dreams smacked our arms, the tubes became swollen, and the spike pierced those purple veins, deliverance from the world. As the plunger drew up a serpent of blood danced into the cloudy liquid, a hit first time, the plunger pushed this chemical dream out of the syringe into my arm, her arm, we trembled Arrr...warmth radiated up the arm rushing into the catacombs which were minds now one... this heat permeated the entirety of our body. We welcomed the Kingdom; the stigmata on our arms were those of a Beat beatitude. Elise wrote:

Oh that I was a
Cunt of golden pleasure more pure
than heroin or heaven.

Trigilio (2014) p.84.

The Cellar.

The origins of 'New Woman' are in Chernyshevsky (1863) *What is to be Done* personified as Sonia Pavlovna. She fled her family believing it to be dark and damp like a cellar. In a similar manner Elise made what a revolutionary move was for a young woman of

nineteen from an upper-class Jewish family with a definite Zionist agenda. Joyce Johnston (2006) *Minor Characters* articulated Elise's situation as she moved out of the family 'cellar':

Nineteen-year-old-girls did not leave home except for dormitories or marriage. If you lived free; you could not expect to live well.

Johnston (2006) p.63.

Existential psychiatry understood the roots of oppression and indeed the roots of insanity in the bourgeois family as David Cooper (1974) *The Death of the Family* wrote:

We don't need Mother and Father anymore. All we need is mothering and fathering…

Blood is thicker than water only in the sense of being the vitalizing stream of social stupidity.

Cooper (1974) pp. 29-30.

Gilly rolled me a huge joint of rich green marijuana just as Allen Ginsberg had rolled one for Elise; we had both inhaled deeply and demonstratively. I had been 'underground', a 'missing minor' for some time. It was time for me to go down to the U.K version of Haight Ashbury in San Francisco, which was Notting Hill Gate in London, the hub of the counter-culture with the offices of Release, a drugs agency always willing to get you checked over by a 'cool' doctor. Hitched down the M1 from near Warwick University and got a 'lift', a lorry driver, a pleasant man. He asked when I last ate, then gave me his sandwich box and asked me my age, which was thirteen, I said 17. He dropped me at Newport Pagnell Services M1 brought me a meal and split. A brown Rover 2000 picked me up; the cat had his suit jacket hanging from a hook:

'Where are you going.' he asks.
'London, man.'

I wore a red tee shirt, green jeans, desert boots and had a shoulder-bag made by my older sister as a present: 'I couldn't wait until you'd done your first trip' she said.

'I can drop you off wherever you want to go.'
'Err, possibly not man. Just where the motorway ends, thanks.'
'Have you been to any good orgies lately?'
A shiver of fear shot through my frame:
'No man, they're not my scene.'

We drove in silence to North London; I could tell he was no novice at this as we pulled into some run down garages. He stopped the car, unzipped his trousers, a little erect penis glared at me.

'Wank me off.'
'No, I don't want to.'
'I can get you as much heroin as you want.'
I didn't believe him, grabbed the door handle and ran.
He shouts:
'I killed someone last week for not doing it.'
Years later I reflected that it was fortunate cars did not come equipped with central locking in the early 1970s.

It was impossible to seek refuge in any way with the police, they were the 'enemy' as well when you're carrying drugs, a set of 'works'[3] and on the run.

We had left these ostensibly 'nice people' for very genuine reasons, it just made sense:

The Cowens were what my parents would call a nice family.

Johnston (2006) p.54.

With a 'nice' apartment, 'nice possessions', nice and empty lives just like my parents and they were also similar in that:

They raised their voices, though, a great deal.

Mr. Cowen was given to threats and rages, Mrs Cowen to tears and recriminations.

Johnston (2006) p.55.

My mother had been telling me she was going to 'commit suicide' since I was seven, since my sister became a hippie and run away from home. They put her in an 'approved school' to which I was taken as a child, it seemed friendlier than home. I was marked as if with a branding iron. Later she was put in a psychiatric hospital both of us apparently insane, but no one else knows the chill of a cellar and the fear of a fist until you experience them. She didn't have the same interest in books; I think that is what saved me. Families can indeed seem like cellars from which we and many like us fled in fear. You go, break the chains or you would be processed by their huge machine Moloch as Ginsberg *Howl* (2014) warned against. Some of us were not ready to be butchered in their abattoir,

---

[3] Underground idiolect for a syringe.

but we knew that the cemetery beckoned, our names
already carved upon the tombstones.

Jehovah and other men.

[I've tried]

I've tried
Been tried
I'll try again
Although my Beings weak
There's nothing worth
But God & you
And God has gone to sleep.
Trigilio (2014) p.49

There seemed to be three significant males prowling in Elise's life, all of them were Jewish like Elise and so they shared some concepts. Inevitably the God Jehovah as she was brought up in an upper middle class Jewish family. Although many Jewish émigrés embraced working class 'resistance ideologies' Anarchism in the case of Emma Goldman and Alexander Berkman which lead to an attempted assassination of the company director Mr. Frick in 1912. Allen Ginsberg's childhood was dominated by the American Communist Party and his mother's descent into insanity. I note, although Elise met Leo Skir at the Hechalutz Hazard camp in 1949, both of them rejected Zionism and Elise re-examined her spiritual inheritance in her poetry and practice. The second man as far as I can ascertain was Mr. Cowen, another patriarch and the third was the major Beat poet Allen Ginsberg. She was afraid of the first two and fell in love with the third. Elise attempted to reject the phallocentric nature of post-war American culture in particular the God of her childhood who cast a shadow of fear over her life, the darkest of nights. She picks up a pen and writes:

Jehovah-

I don't believe a Word
No, I don't believe you care anymore
Do you really want our fear rather than our love?
Trigilio (2014) p 42.

Ginsberg, (Miles 2010, p 172) mentioned, was trying to deny his homosexuality at the time they met. Maybe that was a strand within the thread of her infatuation for the Beat poet. Ginsberg never seemed to say 'no' to very much he thought would deepen his experience or expand his consciousness [he also fought a long battle with various strains of hepatitis]. She went from being an outsider at Colombia University who then had an affair with a philosophy professor to being given the nickname 'Beat Alice' during 1953 because of her new involvement in Bohemian circles.

I became 'another man' in Elise Cowen's life. Influenced by the male Beat writers like William S. Burroughs, Allen Ginsberg and Jack Kerouac from an early age embracing the latter's belief in 'first thought, first word' in my writing. The pen and syringe were handed from their generation to the generation of 1967 and then to my contemporaries. Also, I shared their philosophical proclivities in particular their strand of Existentialism: Nietzsche, Camus and Sartre. I embraced the Sisyphean moment, but Existentialism once realized can only be lived as practice, Praxis, because Camus (1976) *The Myth of Sisyphus* argued that once Nietzsche had announced the 'death of God':

There is but only one serious philosophical problem and this is suicide.

Camus (1976) p.11.

It is possible, I would argue, to perceive this very clearly in Elise, but also its ramifications for humanity in this post-modernist epoch. Click, my tape recording cuts in:

Revolutionary socialist current around Trotsky was in retreat, numerically tiny because of the betrayals of Stalinism and reformist

Socialist Democracy the world became disorientated. Consumerism could never fulfil human needs and there were no other metanarratives.'

Elise and her friends were in a storm without an eye, the rebels who had to make their own cause. Or so it might have appeared, but, Trotsky (1981) *Art and Literature* understood there is never a linear line in literature; the dialectic exists to be answered by its antithesis. Literature cannot achieve that dialectical leap to a higher form of revolutionary literature without a movement lead by the 'universal class', the proletariat. Allen Ginsberg understood something of this:

Holy the Fifth International.

Ginsberg (2014) p.28.

But his International to replace the Fourth International created by Trotsky could not attain its objectives by a dissident aestheticism, a new decadent movement which conjured up Baudelaire and 'art for art's sake' would not suffice. Elise would not have read Marx in depth, but her girlfriend Shelia, before the relationship with Ginsberg, had urged upon her return from Paris:

Another French Revolution was necessary "blood must flow in the streets."

Skir (1970) p.10.

Elise merely commented about the necessity of cheap drugs, Leo Skir recalled. Her disorientation was increased, spinning like a whirling top out of control as she descended further into psychosis and addiction.

Elise's middle name Nadir meant 'nothing and nothingness' and she would have been aware of the pun on Jean-Paul Sartre *Being and Nothingness* (Kaufmann, 1969) as much of the 'Beat' scene was inspired by Existentialist philosophy. However, I was only to enter Elise's magical and dark world upon reading Knight (2006) and then I embarked on an odyssey which is achieving fruition in writing this piece of Life-Writing, I had almost lost my heart to this strange woman and certainly we were rather like twin meteors ablaze in a dark universe. Joyce Johnson, interviewed 3rd October 2002, said of Elise Cowen:

The world treated her very badly because she was an odd girl. She didn't care about being pretty. She was, you know, very bright, and she was eccentric.

Grace and Johnson (eds) (2004) p. 198.

'I'm waiting for the man.'

I recollect living in squalid flat where The Velvet Underground and Nico L.P with the track 'I am waiting for the man', from their 1967 album, was played as if it were a Psalm. The song is about 'scoring' heroin and amphetamine, Elise must have waited for the man many times 'first thing you learn is you always have to wait' (Reed 2008, p. 3) lyrics continued. Elise would always be waiting for Allen Ginsberg and another futile wait that would be. Ginsberg's written choice of phrase, after her death, 'the intellectual madwoman' to describe Elise illustrates his lack of commitment to her. during their relationship Elise typed Ginsberg's long poem about his mother *Kaddish*. Joyce Johnston, Elise's best friend, encapsulated this in (2006) *Minor Characters: a Beat Memoir:*

Elise was a moment in Allen's life. In Elise's, Allen was an eternity.

Johnston (2006) p.78

Allen was, (Miles 2010, pp. 174-5) acting on the recommendations of his analyst who believed his homosexuality to be pathological and therefore encouraged him to have sexual relationships with women. Allen would soon fall in love with Peter Orlovsky, who became a lifelong partner.

Sigmund says...

Elise was Skir (1970) informs us interested in Freud as were the other Beat writers. Burroughs famously 'analysing' Ginsberg, whic was possibly traumatic for both of them. What did Freud say about the nature of the creative process in writers?

A strong experience in the present awakens in the creative mind a memory of an earlier experience (usually belonging to his childhood) from which there now proceeds a wish which finds its fulfilment in the creative work. The work itself exhibits elements of the recent provoking occasion as well as the old memory.

Freud (1964) p.130

Freud compared the whole process to daydreaming. All of us and the Beats had concoctions allowing inner exploration. We all altered states of consciousness either to a lesser extent with hashish or marijuana or a greater extent with L.S.D or as Elise liked Peyote will recognise these. Certainly in the creative person these can be far more intense. The hallucinogens produced, under favourable conditions an insight into the nature of oneself and the natural world or beyond, this was 'a good trip'. The 'bad trip' resembled something more like a descent into a Dantesque inferno. Lysergic acid diethylamide mimicked some of the experiences that are aspects of an untreated psychosis and as in the psychotic state the affected person can understand these as enlightening or intensely frightening. Often over time it is like a marriage of heaven and hell as with all mental illnesses and addiction or any substance misuse. For Elise these were a series of engagements with hell.

The Last Trip

A haze began to encircle us, with the desire to transcend this world and embrace an essence, something the 'elders' did not possess, ignited again within us. Two outcasts of the system, but within us burnt a love of the 'Idea'. We chose to live on the periphery, which is the body of Isis when she is pregnant with the 'Word'. A prophet of this tribe, Ginsberg, said he would give us 'Californian Sunshine' [L.S.D] for an 'ontological awakening.', but he hadn't intended that it should be taken intravenously. He cruised back later on; the sacrament was laid silently in a sea of shadows, solitary in its wrapping of tin foil, awaiting an awakening, its benediction. Elise and I welcomed him, it was really his Mass, it is here she will celebrate the 'Word', the creative energy of the universe which comes from, the feminine, the Lunar Muse, Graves (1984) *The White Goddess*. Elise gently unwrapped the square of tin foil with long pale fingers and held it in her hands, Ginsberg raised it before his forehead and said in words similar to a priest as he holds the Eucharist: 'This is my body, take it and eat, you will be sustained by its vibrations and given a glimpse of infinity.' Elise and I genuflected before the Host, the Word:

'Have a good trip, never forget me.' Ginsberg waved goodbye.

We were dizzy with anticipation as the sweet aroma of Isis scented our crash-pad. We quickly found the dream machine, prepared the 'gear' for a fix and located the mainline... wham without the fear of flying, we were left dancing. A spectre of William Blake appeared in the corner reciting: 'Hear the voice of the bard! Who Present, Past & Future, sees; whose ears have heard The Holy Word that walked among the ancient trees.' Tangerine lights merged into purple clocks which climbed the walls, their disembodied smiles swirled into seas of lemon, lime green flowers melt and kissed the skin, and then the mind dissolved into a pool of turquoise which wept back into the ceiling. They found me eight hours later curled into a ball, repeating a mantra:

'My name is Oedipus; my name is Oedipus, no more psychoanalysis'.

Elise had already been admitted into Bellevue Hospital chanting:

'My name is Electra, my name is Electra, no my name is Emily, Emily Dickinson.'

Emily Dickinson

Elise had written three poems which referenced Emily Dickinson: *Emily, Emily, white witch of Amherst* and *I took the skins of corpses:*

Emily

Emily,
Come summer
You'll take off your
jewelled bees
Which sting me
I'll strip off my stinking
jeans
Hand in hand
We're run outside
Look straight at
the sun
A second time
And get tan.
Trigilio (2014) p.26.

Elise originally concluded her poem with the line: 'And we'll hatch.' She crossed out this line in her notebook (Trigilio 2014, p. 134) either an earlier rejection of motherhood as a choice of a woman Beat poet or possibly a reflection on an unwanted pregnancy with a drunken artist in California (Skir 1970, p. 8). This should have been a D&C but because of the long Christmas vacation the doctors performed a hysterectomy. The poem did suggest a feminist separatism, a sisterhood, which found a voice in the Feminist radicalization of the late 1960's and 1970's.

Thanatos

Elise like I didn't choose not to conform we just couldn't maybe we were too ill, the society we lived in was like a huge Praying mantis and in the end 'hip friends' disengaged. The Freudian opposite of the Pleasure Principle *Eros,* the death instinct *Thanatos* was very powerful in us both. Here a quote from Kay (Elise) as a young woman university drop-out [she did go back and Majored in Modern Poetry] in her friend Joyce Johnston's *Come and Join the Dance*, the first woman Beat novelist published in 1961:

'Well, I think I am going to be a failure," Kay said slowly.
"I think that's already settled. And that's alright. But I want to be a magnificent one. A gigantic smoking ruin.'

Johnston (2014) p 48.

I was similar, but met exceptional therapists and nurses and with modern medicines can write and study. Chipmunkapublishing and The Open University have become like paths through the desert which has led to a more fruitful life. The British philosophy David Hume thought people weren't a consistent 'Self', but rather a 'bundle of selves' like actors playing different parts on the stage of a theatre at various times. Elise would write poignantly:

Did I go mad...? [Extract]

'Did I go mad in my mother's womb?
Waiting to get out
…
On my brain are welts from
the moving that never moves

On my brain are the welts

from the endless stillness

I don't want to intone

"See how she suffers"

"See how she suffers"

(The sting of eyes reminds)

That not really, or only what

I mean-among other things I am not

permitted to feel that much

…

'tick tock'

'But that the truth I guess of

(Even were I to KNOW it)

IS EVERYONE'S…

Knight (2006) pp. 163-164.

Elise Cowen took her place with poets Sylvia Plath and Anne Sexton, women who had attacked the citadel of Patriarchal society, but as a consequence were cast into an abyss of the Great Patriarch. Self-destruction is a product of Patriarchal Capitalism and only mass proletarian revolution can create the conditions for the emancipation of poets, a golden dawn so sweetly scented with love's aroma. This maybe communism as envisaged by women writers like Alexandra Kollontai (1982) *Love of Worker Bees* in these circumstances Elise and I would not be stung by barbed wasps and we would live in a great hive together with the worker-poet's Queen Bee. We would write our poems with pens that have honey for ink and sup happily upon these sweet words. We would be humming with poetry, rather than buzzing with Benzedrine. Maybe I was inculcated with the revolution as a child, but who knows, who remembers? I do. My poem about Elise:

Elegy for Elise Cowen (1933-1962).

Your smile is bright with magic, it draws in verse
To glimpse the "straights", their vision is blurred
And gazes inert, that form is carried in a hearse,
But you who danced the naked poetics preferred

The peace of wombs, the warmth, you "rush" induced
seductress,
Our wastes are frozen with promises, caught and
chosen,
This moth of candle and flame is burnt and wingless,
At dawn you cupped it in a hand and have then written

A dirge of deserts and biting sand which sings
Into the syringe, enchantment of the finite "fix"
Lies with accusations on pages scribed in blotted
words,
This sacred insanity is vibrating your soul, a matrix

For jewels, the wind whispered opiate kiss, it is
In here, where belief lies on the periphery, the poetry
Ascends in grace with those of Auschwitz,
You stumble across the graveyards and weep in
symmetry.

                                        Pearce (2015) p 66.

Bibliography

Camus, A (1976 [1955]) *The Myth of Sisyphus*, Harmondsworth: Penguin Modern Classics.

Cassady, C (1990) *Off the Road: Twenty Years with Cassady, Kerouac and Ginsberg*. London: Flamingo.

Chernyshevsky, N (1983 [1863]) *What is to be Done, New* York: Cornell University Press.

Cooper, D (1974) *The Death of the Family*, Harmondsworth: Pelican books.

Freud, S (1964 [1959]) 'Creative Writing and Daydreaming.' The *Standard Edition of the Complete Psychological Works of Sigmund Freud, Vol 9*, London: The Hogarth Press.

Ginsberg, A (2014 [1956]) *Howl and Other Poems*, San Francisco: City Lights.

Grace, Nancy. M and Johnson, Ronna. C (2004) *Breaking The Rules Of Cool: Interviewing and Reading Women Beat Writers*, Mississippi: The University of Mississippi Press.

Graves, R (1984 [1961]) *The White Goddess*, London: Faber&Faber.

Kaufmann, W (1969) *Existentialism from Dostoevsky to Sartre*, Ohio: Meridian Books.

Kerouac, J (2000 [1957]) *On the Road*, Harmondsworth: Penguin Modern Classics.

Knight, B (2006) *Women of the Beat Generation: the writers, artists and muses at the heart of a revolution*, Berkley: Conart Press.

Kollontai, A (1982 [1932*]) Love of Worker Bees*, London: Virago

Johnston, J (2006) *Minor Characters: a Beat Memoir*, London: Methuen.

Johnston, J (2014[1961]) *Come and Join the Dance*, New York: Open Road.

Miles, B (2010) *Allen Ginsberg Beat Poet*, Great Britain: Virgin Books.

Neale, D. (ed.) (2009) *A Creative Writing Handbook*, Milton Keynes/London: A & C Black in association with The Open University.

Pearce, N (2015) *Icarus Rising: New and Selected Work*, London: Chipmunkapublishing.

Reed, L (2008) *Pass Thro Fire: The Collected Lyrics*, U.S.A: Da Capo Press.

Sartre, J-P (1976[1943]) *Being and Nothingness,* London: Methuen & Co Ltd.

Skir, L She was Beat with Allen Ginsberg: Elise Cowen: a brief memoir of the fifties, *Every Green Review, October 1970.*

Thomas, D (1972) *Collected Poems 1934-1952*, London: Dent & Sons Ltd.

Trigilio, T (2014) *Elise Cowen Poems and Fragments*, Idaho: Asharta Press.

Trotsky, L (1981) *Art and Literature*, New York: Pathfinder Press.

On Method

Richard Holmes argues Life Writing has been profoundly transformed:

People often suggest that the future of biography lies in a radical change of form- in the development of fractured or post-modern narrative models. But this has been going on for quite a time. Peter Achroyd's original version of Dickens (1988) with its flamboyant insertions of fiction.

Cline and Angier (2014) p 118.

My interest was stimulated by Virginia Woolf's 'the lives of the obscure' (Lee (2009) p. 126). Lee continues:

Biographies often speak for the alternative 'hidden lives', especially women's...- grew out of a feminist interest in 'hidden lives'...and of working-class history.

Lee (2009) p. 127.

Although sympathetic to these perspectives my methodology is derived from Marx:

In the social production of their life, men enter into definite relations that are indispensable and independent of their will, relations of production which correspond to a definite stage of production.

Solomon (1979) p. 29.

There were three texts which were seminal in 'Life Writing' *Dead Beat*. Jean Rhys (1981) *Smile Please* which provided a material base for my episodic approach, Janet Frame (1984*) Janet Frame: An Autobiography* that blazed a path for the writing about mental health issues and thirdly, William S. Burroughs (2008) *Junky* which announced the historical moment that allowed people to write honestly about hard drugs.

My method is derived from the practice of Life Writing as outlined in Haslam, H and Neale, D (2009) *Life Writing* and complexified in both Hermione Lee (2009) *Biography: A Very Short Introduction* and more recently in Cline, S and Angier, C (2014) *Life Writing; A Writers & Readers Companion.* Therefore, I am aware of the requirements of an opening paragraph elucidating one's motivation and the academic 'justification' for embarking on the manuscript. Also, I was made aware of the necessity of grounding the text in history, but also of the post-modernist breaking-up of simple narratives and a tendency towards the subverting of the genre. While Neale, D. (ed.) (2009) *A Creative Writing Handbook* taught me important lessons about Aristotelian poetics generally, the use of the dramatic method to enhance prose and the effective use of dialogue. Hence my idiolect is appropriate to the historical sense of 'place', the 'Beat Generation' and the 'counter-culture'. I 'cross-cut' in some sections and also merge narratives. The usage of quasi- Roman Catholic metaphor is consistent with Jack Kerouac's usage of 'Beat' 'beatitude' which I extend in 'The Last Trip' to the Eucharistic: 'Take you all of this and eat' as metaphors for the consummation and consumption of the L.S.D. This surreal employment of language is entirely congruent with the 'altered state of consciousness' which it describes. Sergei Eisenstein's montage technique is used in, for instance, the descriptions of the family by Sonia Pavlovna, the biographical detail of the Cowen family and mine with Cooper's reflection on the redundancy of the family, which 'cuts' to a verbatim account of what happened when I hitchhiked down to London as a young adolescent. All of these linguistic, dramatic and cinematic devices were vital in allowing me to compose my manuscript, *Dead Beat.* The title is a play on words as in the premature death of a 'beat poet' and the now archaic American phrase 'dead-beat' i.e. exhausted. The authorial voice in my text is 'first-person plural.'

In regard of the Aristotelian poetic *Poetics* (Aristotle 1996) I employ a 'dramatic arc' which articulates 'the whole':

'A whole is that which has a beginning, a middle and an end.'

Aristotle (1996) p.13.

There is a causal relationship between each section which I disrupt, writing *in medias res*. Neale (2009) comments on autobiography as a genre even when it is 'subverted':

... character is still it's most central and essential feature, just as in the more straightforward Robinson Crusoe.

Neale (2009) p.7.

Aristotle's concept was developed by Freytag (2004) and illustrated in Fig 3:

Fig.3
Freytag's Pyramid

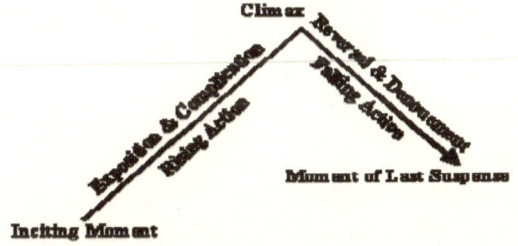

I employ this structure and the conflicts which generate the 'action' are numerous e.g. familial and ideological. I recalled *The Hours* (Neale 2009, pp 350-54) and make use of Time and emblematic imagery, e.g. drug images. I use parallel stories; Elise Cowen's and mine with the same plot. Forster commented on the relationship between the story and the plot:

The king died and then the queen died. The king died and then the queen died of grief.

Forster (1955) p.86.

The difference between the two, he argued, was the plot has a causal nature in an Aristotelian sense. A submerged and ordered sequence of action that creates a 'plot.'

I would suggest that as a result of studying A363 I have learnt to embrace 'the freedom of form'. I now have a far greater repertoire of technical devices and know better how to articulate my imagination. This is tantamount and consistent with asserting the module has allowed me to develop a 'creative voice'.   One invaluable lesson learnt was the discipline of Realism in a 'stage-drama'. As I was engaged with a concrete situation and compelled to physically move my characters upon a stage my abstraction had to be rooted in a material base. This was not a limiting experience, quite the opposite and with the use of Brecht's 'alienation effect' I was able to subvert Naturalism when I choose. Elizabeth Bishop correctly maintains of poetic 'forms': 'They seem to start the machinery.' (Neale 2009, p. 246).

However, once learnt 'form' can be subverted as Elise Cowen and the Beat writers on the West Coast of America and the confessional' writers of the East Coast Establishment exhibited with consummate ability. The 'formal' and the 'experimental' can only complement. Is this not the paradox of modernism and post-modernism, the Metaphysical poets and Romanticism, and the debates about 'alienation effect' and Formalism in Socialist Realism which continue in Marxist circles? These apparent paradoxes are in fact dialectical in nature and each must therefore yes, contain a contradiction, but also a 'unity of opposites' which must then create the dialectical leap to a higher stage, 'the negation of the negation' as delineated by Engels (1976) *Dialectics of Nature*:

The law of the transformation of quantity into quality and vice versa; The law of the interpenetration of opposites; The law of the negation of the negation.
Engels (1976) p.62.

This is not a metaphysical Hegelian aesthetic, but rather one rooted in the production and reproduction of everyday life, the material creation of literature. Thus the theoretical 'argument' that underpins my piece of Life Writing is that the Beat Generation as a social phenomenon could not produce the objective material or subjective conditions necessary for an Aristotelian *eudemonia* for outsider poets under capitalism. These poets like Elise and I would, it seems, only find creative fulfilment and emotional solace under the conditions of communism. I have not 'foregrounded' this as my tutor warned against an overly academic style. I have attempted to write balanced creative non-fiction as appropriate to Life Writing.

Bibliography

Aristotle (1996) *Poetics*, London: Penguin Classics.

Burroughs, William. S (2008 [1953]) *Junky*, London: Penguin Classics.

Cline, S and Angier, C (2014) *Life Writing; A Writers & Readers Companion*. London: Bloomsbury.

Engels, F (1976 [1883]) *Dialectics of Nature*, Moscow: Progress Publishers.

Forster. E. M (1955 [1927]) *Aspects of the Novel*, Harcourt, Brave & World: New York.

Frame, J (1984) *Janet Frame: An Autobiography*, London: The Women's Press.

Freytag (2004 [1863]) *Technique of the Drama: An Exposition of Dramatic Composition and Art*, Hawaii: University Press of the Pacific

Haslam, H and Neale, D (2009) *Life Writing*, London: Routledge in association with The Open University

Lee, H (2009) *Biography: A Very Short Introduction*, Oxford: Oxford University Press.

Neale, D. (ed.) (2009) *A Creative Writing Handbook*, Milton Keynes/London: A & C Black in association with The Open University

Rhys, J (1981) *Smile Please: An Autobiography*, Harmondsworth: Penguin Books.

The Swallow

The leaves began to brood into autumnal red, crisp crimson just before the frost bites when she, a swallow, fluttered in through an open window they had forgotten to close. You could now peer into another nest of nails. She noticed there was a shattered pane in a smaller room. However the main room seemed perfectly ordered, a black leather three piece suit, a proud wooden cabinet which contained a colour television, a dark brown wall to wall carpet, a door ajar gave a glimpse of a dark tan dining table. There were not the vying aromas of the poor, the really poor part of this city: in a word, it was 'bourgeois'. Or like a Ford factory canteen replicated in every Ford factory across the world. 1972 and The Blitzkrieg Man seemed an unhappy man she noted. Why? Of course, his world was like a ball on fire, a conflagration from Saigon to Chicago from Grosvenor Square to Stuttgart. There was the Viet-Ming, the Black Panthers, that Tariq Ali and the Baader-Meinhof Gang or as some would say, 'Red Army Faction'. He believed it to be victimization, a digression of Eve, of Pandora, she guessed. There was no shelter for him as he could not do as Jagger spewed out while gyrating like a little demon seeking oblivion in Gimme Shelter three years earlier she heard:

"Gimme shelter come on give me shelter, it's just a fix away, it's just a hit away."

Immediately the swallow realized he was as straight as a rod of iron and as stiff as the ruler he measured everyone and everything by. She saw swooping about that he seeks that inflated reflection of himself in the looking-glass which reflects his bourgeois wife as Virginia Woolf had explained in that little book which promised so much. Those pages lay open in her mind now. Like all who fly she knew that mirrors break and should not be stared at and spotted a crumpled invitation to that curved psychedelic groove which is etched in the mind by Lysergic Acid hiding in the corner. Yes 'acid', a method of psychological exploration, for some it burnt through the mind like a hot knife through butter, leaving it melted, a splodge. Timothy Leary hadn't anticipated that.

Eva lay flat out on the floor blooded, she observed, but absorbed blood like a sponge soaks-up spilt red wine. Eva staggered and seemed to her inspired with the primordial fertility of the first monthly curse, the first towel-less, pad-less, tampon-less bleed remembered by every woman, each generation. She straightened herself and spat out these words between her swollen lower and throbbing upper lips:

'Go on, why don't you hit me again just to make yourself feel like a real man?'

Blitzkrieg Man's flash of lightning had hit a lightning conductor; he was earthed by the audacity of his wife the swallow imagined he thought that as a gentleman, he wouldn't hit a woman. Not the fairer sex who must be put on a pedestal and admired, that is for men like Blitzkrieg Man until they stepped down from the pedestal and became human... impossible, for him to knock a woman off her pedestal. He seemed to her capable of deafening self-delusion as most people expected the sun to raise and set:

'But my dear you have cut your lip again, do take more care... Here, take this handkerchief.'said The Blitzkrieg Man.

'Just another male chauvinist pig, you just oink bloody oink, you honky motherfucker'. Brigitte, his ex-student daughter, yelled.

'Not all that again young lady. You are a pathological liar. I am a doctor so I do know the symptoms of nervous disorders, maladies of the mind, I will say it "psychiatric illness". Now the inside of an admission unit can become quite, what should I say, busy, you wouldn't like that, now would you.'

The swallow watched as she grabbed her Little Red Book, a whirlwind unleashing:

'Mao says: "Political power comes out of the barrel of a gun."'

'You will respect your mother and father as well as your country I say,

I insist.' He said like a robot that saw cold steel and salivated iron fillings.

Fluttering she observed him writing on the wax tableau of his mind… what would happen if everyone did what Jagger and Leary advocated. There had been a growing amount of research into this so-called, what a pretension, 'counterculture', the Nation would grind to a halt. Of course, there was one Nation, just one happy family, not everyone could lunge around dreaming like drop outs. NO! All must work and boost G.N.P; (there he stood a gross national product she thought). After all someone had said, he pencilled a murmur of a memory, 'Arbeit macht frei'. He mouthed the words in carefully pronounced and refined English 'work makes you free'. Yes of course and what else could it do, Ford proved at their Dagenham Plant, symmetry is aesthetic perfection when it comes to the factories. She noted his nib slipped 'cemeteries'.

Eva had cleaned her mouth, applied the usual cosmetic necessaries, an abused bourgeois woman would use the term 'necessaries' the swallow knew and walked back into the living room, 'a death chamber' she sighed. This was the death of love and death of the family. Just one veiled glance towards Brigitte that hoped for a new dawn with her daughter's generation. That masked smile told the swallow this talk of revolution was a little extreme, but so was the clenched fist in the mouth from someone who cannot recall what he has done:

'She's young and an idealist, you shouldn't be so hard on her.' enjoined Eva.

'Me, hard on anyone, ironic isn't it. I go out to work, support you all and have a daughter claiming I have a resemblance to a piece of pork.'

These decomposing nests were sub-atomic particles of the atom that was suburbia, the atom had split and its flames and hurricanes consumed Nagasaki and Hiroshima. The words had already been fashioned into a semi-circle of wrought iron 'Arbeit macht frei' above the entrance of Auschwitz. Then the swallow remembered her mother, a 'mental-defective', with the black triangle sown onto her blue and white striped uniform, herded into Auschwitz from the cattle-tracks with the Jewish people, the communists and homosexuals. That was when she had escaped the womb and became a swallow.

She dived down and spotted a copy of Hermann Hesse Steppenwolf opened at the page which described a door with the sign: 'For madmen only'. She, the swallow, had read Freud and embroiders this text which is sown into your mind with invisible thread:

"Dreams are the royal road to the unconscious."

Had Brigitte passed through Hesse's door in a dream? She saw a dark shadow haunted The Blitzkrieg Man. What had it all meant, those had been idle threats towards Brigitte about mental hospitals, and he was only trying to control her as he attempted to restrain a world which was hurtling towards a nemesis for the privileged, its coming is certain but its fruition not, she mused.

She swept toward the end of her song and told that Brigitte was ill in the terms employed by psychiatry, but not by 'anti-psychiatry'. Brigitte had read how the S.P.K argued 'turn illness into a weapon' and that it was a sick society that had caused her malady, her 'illness.' An illusion the swallow had conjured was the story took place in England, yes that is correct, however, in West Germany Brigitte's Double was a member of Sozalistischespatentkolletiv (SPK). Brigitte transmogrified in 1972 from Socialist Patients Collective fledgling to emerge from the chrysalis to become one of the butterflies in the second generation 'Red Army Faction'. Brigitte's German mother had been a swallow. This swallow watched Brigitte pondering Shakespeare:

'I acknowledge this thing of darkness mine.'

Brigitte didn't mess around, muttered Mao: 'we must draw a clear dividing line between ourselves and the enemy.'

She whispered: 'Daddy, I have a little something for you.'

'Yes.'

'I'm going to light your fire baby.' She smiled.

Brigitte then coolly sprayed his bedroom with bullets from her Sten Automatic Pistol and precisely riddled her father with bullets again and again to make him perform a little dance; the bullets jerked his body like stings make a marionette jump. Was it History that had pulled those strings? She produced a Luger pistol placed its cold black barrel on her lap and waited for the 'pigs', the police. Her mother sat silent and stolid. The Sirens wailed, but only lure more into dreams of love which linger behind every bloody sunset. This swallow flew from this chamber knowing that she, those who read Daddy escaped having their hearts pierced by spears of fire as Sylvia's had been. She always had to fly high, higher, circling just to escape that icy stare and glare of Room 101.

Notes on 'The Swallow'

Terrorism' pervades the news almost every day; my narrative is of another milieu, different 'backstory' and ideology. Plath (1985) *Daddy* remained central throughout the editing. The 'swallow' originated in Frame (2008) where Grace Cleave is transmogrified into 'a migratory bird' because of feelings of dissociation. She is a 'personification' of Existentialist freedom. Research included: Meinhoff (1971), Cooper (1972) and S.P.K. (1972). I attempt to answer

Dostoevsky (1864) whose 'Underground Man' was a reply to Chernyshevsky (1863) who created the literary 'New Woman' incarnate in Vera Pavlovna, there is an allusion to Chekhov (1896) in my title. The narrator is the 'swallow'; she's a limited omniscient narrator. This allows the reader to see the world through her eyes and allows her insights into the story, retaining some of the intimacy of the first-person narrator as well as the advantages of a partial omniscience; 'confessional intimacy' with some 'authorial distance'. I tried to employ 'dialogue' for both 'characterization' and changing the 'pace' of my story. There is some 'telling' as befits an instrumentalist story, the conclusion gains momentum by 'showing'. The "crumpled invitation" is an attempt to apply the concept of 'Chekhov's Gun' to 'foreground' Brigitte's madness which also references Dostoevsky *The Double* (1846). Throughout the story I use contradiction and paradox as a strategy to propel the reader's interest and 'defamiliarize' their experience as in dialectical opposed belief systems of Patriarchal Capitalism and a tendency within Western Maoism. I utilize both simile and metaphor in my prose. My intention regarding the resolution of my story is to realize a combination of a 'Chekhovian Ending' with 'Instrumentalism'. Although the genre is Historical Fiction it is subverted by being narrated by 'the swallow' who must question the nature of Realism for she is a non-human narrator. It has a resemblance to the parabolic. The intention was to comment on Patriarchal Capitalism:

"Representation of the world, like the world itself, is the work of men; they describe it from their own point of view, which they confuse with absolute truth."

De Beauvoir (1972) p. 161.

Both Sartre and Simone de Beauvoir were Maoist sympathisers.

References.

Bennett, T (1979) *Marxism and Formalism*, Methuen & Co Ltd: London.

Chekhov, A (1998) [1896]) *Five Plays: Ivanov, The Seagull, Uncle Vanya, Three Sisters, and The Cherry Orchard*, Oxford: Oxford World's Classics.

Chernyshevsky, N (1989 [1863]) *What Is to be Done?* Cornell University Press: Ithaca and London.

Cooper, D (1972) *The Death of The Family*, Harmondsworth: Penguin Books.

De Beauvoir, S (1972) *The Second Sex*, trains. H. M. Parshley, New York: Vintage.

Dostoevsky, F (1985 [1864, 1846]) *Notes from Underground, The Double*, Harmondsworth: Penguin Classics.

Frame, J (2008) *Towards another Summer*, Virago: London.

Meinhoff, U {Red Army Faction} (2009 [1971]) *The Urban Guerrilla Concept*, Montreal: Kersplebedeb Publishing.

Neale, D. (ed.) (2009) *A Creative Writing Handbook*, Milton Keynes/London: A & C Black in association with The Open University.

Plath, S (1985) *Selected Poems*, London: Faber & Faber.

Shakespeare (1998) *The Tempest*, ed Orgel, S. Oxford: Oxford World's Classics. Sozalistischespatentkolletiv (1984 [1972]) *SPK: Turn Illness into a Weapon*, Dresden: Trikont.

Electra Unbound: A Modern Tragicomedy.
The action takes place over 24 hours.

Characters with some minor notes on direction.

Bridget.

A young student dropout, she has aligned herself with the radical currents in Western anti-psychiatry and armed urban Maoism. These occurred in Western Europe during the late 1960's until the late 1970s. She is in custody after killing her father.

Dr. Winston Smith.

A middle-aged male forensic psychiatrist with a particular interest in Jungian psychology and social science.

Police Superintendent Julia Mosley.

A strict disciplinarian.

The Swallow. *[Off stage and illuminated by a spotlight when speaking.]*

She sees all the dramatic action and comments upon it as she swoops in and out. A solitary and atomised Aristotelian Chorus who creates a Brechtian 'alienation effect.'

Eva.

Bridget's mother, traumatized by her daughter's parricide.

Psychiatric nurses and Polices officers *[stock-characters 'doubled' so one actor doubles-up as a good nurse/ good policeman and another as a bad nurse/ bad policeman].*

Locations: A police station. A secure psychiatric ward *[on a split stage].*

A presidium arch stage.

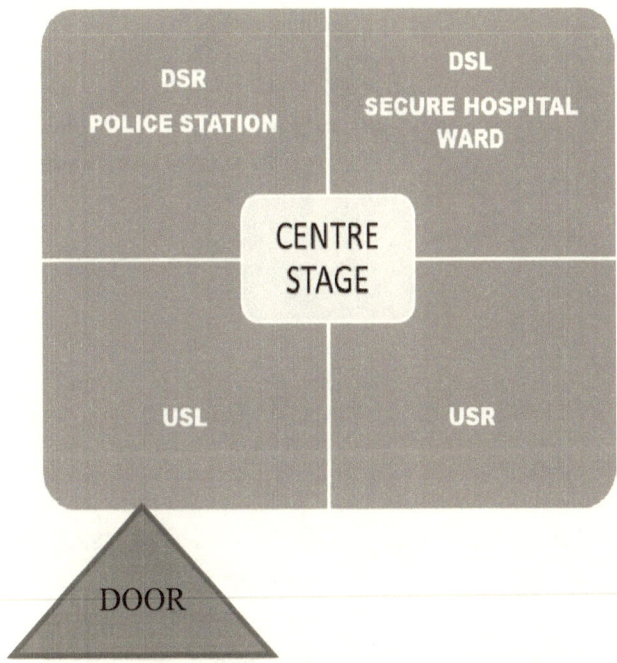

AUDIENCE.

Abbreviations used:

DSL: downstage left, etc. USR: upstage right, etc. [as the actor faces the audience].

CS: 'centre stage.'
Off Stage: literally off stage, but heard on stage.

Freytag's Pyramid

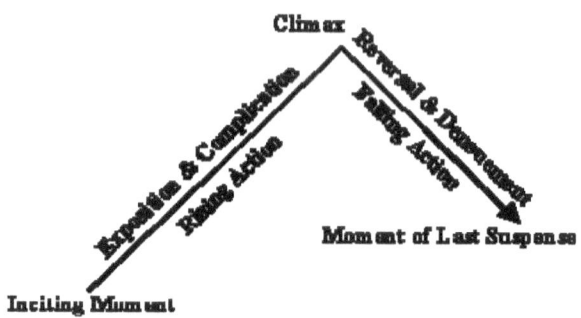

Freytag (1863) model of Aristotelian Tragedy

ACT 1.

Scene 1 A police station, which in not like an ordinary one, but more like 'Paddington Green' which is a British high-security station and holding unit for politically motivated offenders. The officers **have** no visible 'ID' numbers

BRIDGET is roughly bundled onto the stage. USR.

Bridget: Get your filthy pig hands off me

Uniformed police #1: Wouldn't want to touch that scum, she, it, killed her father. Shot the poor bleeder in his bed. What's your name? Are you really human or just a monster that looks like one. Look like a human, you'd have to put a bag over your head for me to fuck it.

(pause)

Officer #2: Come on we have to charge you. I am sorry about the language

Bridget: I will only give my status which is 'international revolutionary' and a brief statement.' I am a sister of the international struggle between the forces of reaction and those of progressive people's liberation movements.'

(pause)

Bridget: I am human only too human[4]. He was the enemy, my father, like it was personified, you know what I mean... He was oppression incarnate.

Officer #2: Another wordy one.

Officer #1: Educated cow. I thought you people were the toiling masses rising up. You seem like a bunch of spoilt kids to me.

Bridget [coldly]: Don't call me 'a spoilt kid'…. I am a revolutionary woman, and I believe like Mao in 'Drawing a clear line between the enemy and ourselves'[5]

There is a struggle during which BRIDGET is wrestled to the floor, face down and her hands handcuffed behind her back. Chairs and tables are overturned

Bridget: You can kill me, but you can't kill an ideal, the movement.

THE SWALLOW through a loudhailer Off Stage:

The pigs think we are scum, but just look and learn. Draw your own conclusions and don't be deceived, I say again, look and learn.

EVA is USL in the psychiatric ward and two nurses are trying to give her sedatives; she is distressed and walking on the spot. They do not speak except to say:

---

[4] Nietzsche, F (1994).
[5] Mao TseTung cited in Meinhoff, U (1971).

Nurse #2: Come on take the medicine you know it's good for you.

Nurse #1: Now you don't want an injection, do you, so take the pills.

Eva: My child...

Scene 2 USL BRIDGET from USR on her feet, but remaining handcuffed.

Lunges towards her mother:

Bridget You have betrayed woman, you made her dependent on 'the Other', the male, the husband, my father. Where is your 'sisterhood', any solidarity? between women? Shit, mother, don't you have a mind of your own. I guess that's a fairly vacuous question in itself.

INSPECTOR JULIA MOSLEY enters CSR [possibly wearing the uniform of the 1930's Mosleyite 'British Union of Fascists' known as the 'Black Shirts'.]

Mosley: The woman is ill; the young bitch is a criminal. Keep them apart and while you are at it rough that little whore up a bit.

The police officer #1 hits Bridget with increasing velocity and rapidity, he is warming to his task.

Bridget: AR, Arrr ah, you filth... not every woman is cruising for a bruising, you are...bloody hell that hurt...the dead.

THE SWALLOW stands-up OFF STAGE and is suddenly illuminated by a bright spotlight. She holds a white placard, which has emboldened upon in bold letters:

FASCIST PIGS.

DR. WINSTON SMITH enters DSL and glides into the melee. He put the upturned furniture back in place and places the papers in their files:

Dr. Winston Smith: The young woman seems irrational yet not in a delirium, I want to look into this a little deeper. Let me spend some time with her.

He then orders that handcuffs be taken off and escorts Bridget to the far edge of the USL.

Scene 3. A secure psychiatric ward is eerily quiet as the patients are so heavily sedated that they forget when they are holding cigarettes. The cigarettes smoulder into fingers   and then fall onto fire-resistant carpets. Dr. Winston Smith and Bridget are sitting in   the seclusion of his office. On his desk is Jung, *The Theory of Psychoanalysis* [6] and Leach's book about Levi-Strauss published in 1970 [7] with *heavy* underlining.   USL

Dr. Winston Smith: Now, I am going to give you a chance as I can see you are an educated woman. I have been reading some Carl Jung about his discovery of the 'Electra Complex'.

---

[6] Jung, C (1998)
[7] Leach, E (1970)

He picks up the book which is heavily underlined:

Bridget: I scribble all over my books as well.

Dr. Winston Smith: Leach argues in a recent study that the message of Greek mythology is simple enough: 'if society is to go on, daughters must be disloyal to their parents and sons must destroy [replace] their fathers'.
(pause)
Yes, well he first mentioned it in 1913, just at the time he was breaking with Freud.

Bridget: Is that a fact...

Dr. Winston Smith: Do I note a trace of irony, of a lack of deference to the analyst.

Bridget: Maybe.

Dr. Winston Smith: So, may I ask what are your beliefs Bridget?

Bridget: I think you have a fairly good idea doctor. Ulrike Meinhoff argues that in the urban conurbations in the West 'the armed struggle is the necessary prerequisite for the proletarian revolution.' I was a member of anti-psychiatry group at a university hospital unit, our doctors became convinced of the position that psychiatric illness was the product of the oppressive relations in society, particularly the family... taught us to become revolutionaries, urban guerrillas.'

Dr. Winston Smith: And you killed your father...

Bridget. He was an agent of social control…. he was a real brute doctor, he would hit my mother and then pretend he had no memory of it.

Dr. Winston Smith: I see, oh dear I see. That is, I cannot see for I am blinded. I have no eyes, like Oedipus Rex.

Bridget: You can 'see' if you want to…. you are part of the system of what Louis Althusser[8] calls the 'Repressive State Apparatus' as a forensic psychiatrist you openly control people and with 'Ideological State Apparatus' as a father in the nuclear family. I am making this apparent because ideology is insidious. It uses 'interpellation' or 'hails' people, they don't see it as 'false consciousness', but as their chosen beliefs, a way of life.

The stage darkens and DR. WINSTON SMITH is bathed in red light

Dr. Winston Smith:[with obvious physical unease] Steady on Bridget…

(pause)

Bridget: Camus says there is only one serious philosophical question after realization; 'suicide or recovery.'

Dr. Winston Smith: You too have read his Myth of Sisyphus?

DR. WINSTON SMITH looks away and stares across the stage.

---

[8] Althusser, L (1971)

The Swallow OFFSTAGE: A game of chess and the King has been placed in check by our Queen.

ACT 2.
Scene 1. CS. INSPSECTOR JULIA MOSLEY:

Winston, why do you go easy on the young thug? She killed her father, which makes her a parricide. Should be hung as far as I am concerned.

 Dr. Winston Smith: She is a complex character, disassociated from reality. Or at least the reality of the majority of people.

Inspector Julia Mosley: Do you remember, before they had us in Room 101 we were lovers, we met secretly. We thought our love was revolutionary.

Dr. Winston Smith: It was, in a fashion, but it is easier to rebel against the morality of a system rather than the system itself.

Inspector Julia Mosley: Easy and it was good Winston, wasn't it…?

(pause)

Good and easy, ah…

INSPECTOR JULIA MOSLEY moves her face towards him, he pulls away.

No, I am sorry, not again Julia.

Damn you.

Swallow [off stage] Star-crossed lovers, no way man.

Scene 2. USL   In DR. WINSTON SMITH's office:

Dr. Winston Smith: Bridget, I am interested in your 'high-functionality', your ability to intellectualize all your problems, it is if you have retreated into that domain.

Bridget: It is a rich land, but I can see where you are going. It has its benefits, but also…. well, I live there, you see.

Dr. Winston Smith: I believe I do, or at least am beginning to understand. Now Bridget, you have helped me to understand the world, my role in it. Bridget, did your parent's show you emotional love, or were it all a matter of material tokens of a love that may or may not have been there.

Bidget [sobbing] 'Love'… what is that… material security but love… they were, are, emotional cripples.

Dr. Winston Smith [takes her hand]: I can guide you out of this illness.

Bridget: What 'illness'.

Scene 3.USL.

BRIDGET paces around Dr. Winston Smith chanting incantations, he is not afraid: Eliminate all rational thought, Eliminate all rational thought, Eliminate all rational thought.

So writes William Burroughs.

(pause)

Don't you see that in an insane world? to quote R. D. Laing 'It is mad to be normal'[9]

Dr. Winston Smith: Eureka Electra, I think I have got it.

Bridget: Cool.

The Swallow [off stage] Solidarity, comrades and lovers.

ACT 3. Evening. Bridget and Eva are now on the secure ward USR. The nurses are hoping for a peaceful night...

Scene 1. BRIDGET moves toward her mother:

Bridget: Mother, you must be strong. They will try and give you shiny white tablets or brown syrup. Don't take it, it is called Chlorpromazine will turn your mind into a rotting turnip and cause your limbs to jerk.

Eva: Why would they do things like that to us, we are patients and the nurse says they only want to help.

Bridget: Mother, they are cogs in a machine. They do what they are told.

—————————————————————

[9]Mullen, B. (1995).

Eva: You really do understand how things are, my child. You are teaching with wisdom that astounds me. For the first time in my life I know what it is to be free. You have changed, beatitude, you remind me of St. Clare and all those 'Poor Clare's' living a life of poverty and serving the poor.

The Swallow [offstage] A mistake, very touching though.

DR WINSTON SMITH ENTERS CSR.

Dr. Winston Smith: Bridget, there is something urgent I need to tell you. Before they got to me I was a person like Winston Smith as in George Orwell's novel '1984'. I was a revolutionary of sorts, a utopian dreamer, but they hammered me and I was re-socialized and became a forensic psychiatrist, I sold out, but I still believe 'if there is hope it lies in the proles.'

Bridget: That is a quote from the novel.

Dr. Winston Smith: Yes, of course I should have expected you to know.

Scene 2.

Bridget: Winston, my comrade. Today's conditions in the Western urban centres must be seen from an internationalist perspective. Vietnam is being bombed, they are using napalm on children.

Dr. Winston Smith: I have seen some of the photographs, it is awful, really terrible.

Bridget: Remember what I said about Ulrike Meinhoff…

(pulse)

Dr. Winston Smith: No that is too much to expect.

Bridget: As Anglia Davis says: 'Revolution is a serious thing, the most serious thing about a revolutionary's life. When one commits oneself to the struggle, it must be for a lifetime.'

Dr. Winston Smith: I am a doctor, I have a family. I couldn't leave them to fend for themselves.

The Swallow offstage: That is a line that must be crossed both Ulrike Meinhoff and Gudrun Ensslin did.

Silence….

Scene3.

Bridget: You will Winston.

She embraces him and they kiss deeply.

Bridget: That is how important the struggle is.

Nurse #2: Bloody hell, they are snogging. The doctor and that woman, the one they brought from the police station earlier.

Nurse #1: Little hussy.

Nurse #2: What should we do?

Nurse #1: They are both going down for a long time, I'm ringing the police.

Inspector Julia enters CSR and produces a small pistol, not a service issue.

Inspector Julia: You have betrayed me, everyone, everything. I will shoot you both dead.

Bridget: We haven't betrayed love or the revolution.

Winston freezes unable to move. Bridget grasps the pistol.

Bridget: Unlike Desdemona I can pronounce the word 'whore' and you are the whore of the bourgeoisie. Take that.

A single shot rings out. Bridget and Winston run across the stage DSR and Bridget kicks open the door. They exit hand in hand. A shower of red rose petals is thrown onto the empty stage DSL by THE SWALLOW and she sings The Internationale…

ON THE PLAY...

For Plato, art is 'shadow of shadows', Aristotle developed a systematic aesthetic:

Tragedy is an imitation of an action that is admirable, complete and possesses magnitude...Virtually all tragedians... use these formal characteristics.... for in fact every drama alike has spectacle, character, plot, diction, song and reasoning. But the most important is structure of events.

Heath (1996) p. 11.

Aristotle wrote what has become a dictum for Western dramatists:

Tragedy, then, is a representation of an action that is worth serious attention, complex in itself, and of amplitude; in language enriched by a variety of artistic devices appropriate to the several parts of the play; presented in the form of actions, not narration; by means of a pity and fear bringing about a purgation of these emotions.

Dorsch (1965) p. 38-39.

Electra Unbound: a Tragicomedy.'s main Aristotelian action is articulated as a dialectical process.   Bridget is a revolutionary who transforms Dr. Winston Smith's *Weltanschauung* while he in turn shows her the love she was denied as a child. It does, however, leave an unanswered question: is she in fact resolving her 'Electra Complex' or not? My drama is an attempt to employ Brechtian 'complex seeing' as defined by Raymond Williams in Aristotelian dramatology:

It is not the good person against the bad, but goodness and badness as alternate expressions of a single being. This is complex seeing and it is deeply integrated with dramatic form.'

Williams (2006) p. 234-235.

This dialectic is enacted within the structure of Aristotelian Tragedy, but with a happy 'turn' at the conclusion transforming it into a tragicomedy. I try to make the play function on a cause-effect basis as Aristotle advised and use the 'dramatic arc' (Neale (2009) p 85). The main technical problem I encountered in transforming TMA01 *The Swallow'* into TMA02 was that of how to incorporate the swallow who had been an omniscient third-person narrator into my drama. I attempted this by making her into an atomized Aristotelian chorus who was off stage, but with a presence, either heard or seen on stage and utilising the methodology of Brecht (2013) *Life of Galileo* where placards are used in Brecht's concept of 'epic theatre' (Brecht, 1964). I attempt to combine both *mimesis* and Brecht's *'Alienation-Effect'.*

The play begins with an allusion to Shelley (2009) *Prometheus Unbound* and ends with one to Ibsen (2008) *A Doll's House.* Bridget's chanting of Burroughs's in Act 2, Scene 3 is an attempt to make language chaotic and thus challenge its phallocentric nature as achieved in the work of Hélène Cixous *'creature feminine'* [feminine writing].

Bibliography

Althusser, L (2008 [1971]) *Ideology and Ideological State Apparatus. (Notes towards an investigation)*, London: Verso.

Aristotle/Horace/Longinus (1965) Classical *Literary Criticism*, trans, T. S. Dorsch, Harmondsworth: Penguin Classics

Aristotle (1996), *Poetics*, trans, Malcolm Heath, Harmondsworth: Penguin Classics.

Brecht, B (1964) *Brecht on Theatre*, trans, John Willett, London: Methuen Drama.

Brecht, B (2006) *Life of Galileo*, trans, John Willett, London: Bloomsbury.

Jung, C (1998) *The Essential Carl Jung*, London, Fontana Books.

Ibsen, H (2008) *Four Major Plays*, Oxford: Oxford World Classics.

Leach, E (1970) *Claude Levi-Strauss*. Revised ed. New York: Viking Press.

Meinhoff, U {Red Army Faction} (2009 [1971]) *The Urban Guerrilla Concept*, Montreal: Kersplebedeb Publishing.

Mullen, B (1995) *Mad To Be Normal: conversations with R. D. Laing*, London: Free Association Books.

Neale, D. (ed) (2009) *A Creative Writing Handbook*, Milton Keynes/London: A & C Black in association with The Open University.

Nietzsche, F (1994 [1878]) *Human, All Too Human*, Harmondsworth: Penguin Classics.

Orwell. G (1983) [1949]) *Nineteen Eighty- Four*, Harmondsworth: Penguin Books.

Shelley (2009) The Major Works, Percy Bysshe Shelley, Oxford, Oxford World's Classics

Williams, R (2006[1964]) *Modern Tragedy*, Canada: boardview encore editions.

What is literature?

Roman Jacobson maintained:

'Literature is organized violence committed on everyday language.'

Jacobson, Roman in Eagleton, Terry:

The question 'what is literature?' is a literary device in that it is a rhetorical question, it elicits an answer. I shall argue or sketch a number of well-established replies and allow you to reach your own conclusions.

Literature and poetry can be differentiated from other writing or speech by having the quality of 'literariness'. This term was first employed by the Russian Formalist critic Roman Jacobson in 1919 when he declared:

The subject of literary scholarship is not literature in it's totality, but literariness, that is, that which makes a given work of literature.

Jacobson, Roman [1919] in Victor Erlich (1981) p, 171, Russian Formalism; History – Doctrine, Yale University Press.

So for the Russian Formalists literature was not the incarnation of: The best that has been thought and said in the world.

Arnold, Mathew ([1869] (1971) Culture and Anarchy, p, 6. Cambridge University Press

Some kind of secular religion as Mathew Arnold argued, would save Western capitalist civilization from both the creeping philistinism of the rising bourgeoisie and the degeneration of the masses and that this may bring about social disorder. Arnold was hoping to make cultural glue, a kind of cultural opium of the people. It would by implication require a transcendental quality inherent in an ether of eternal 'Ideas'. The Canon of bourgeois texts is to be read with the guiding hand of a bourgeois curriculum e.g. 'The Newbolt Report'.

However, there was disagreement between the Russian Formalists who deviated from the concept held by most other Marxists that literature was simply a reflection in the ideological superstructure of the material base of any given socio-economic epoch, 'in the last instant.' The views of the Formalists were unorthodox although most remained close to the ideas of the Bolshevik revolution and their ideas around them which went out of favour with the rise of the Stalinist counter-revolution. Leon Trotsky learning from and leaning towards the Russian Formalists claimed artistic creation is:

A deflection, a changing and transformation of reality, in accordance with the particular laws of art.

Trotsky, Leon (1924) Literature and Revolution in Eagleton, Terry Marxism and Literary Criticism (2002), p. 46 Routledge.

The key to understanding the ideas of the Formalists lies in this concept of 'literariness'. They argued that in everyday language and literature we develop habits or are 'automatized' by the routine of everyday life. We simply may not notice literature when we are reading it because of it does not possess this quality of 'literariness'. What gives something, a material text, this quality? It is 'defamiliarization' argued Victor Shklovsky in an important text, *Poetry as Technique* (1917) and this is central to the ripening of the human experience:

'Art exists that one may recover the sensation of life… The purpose of art is to impart the sensation of things as they are perceived not as they are known.'

Shklovsky, Victor (1917) Poetry as Technique in Hans Bertens (2008) Literary Theory. p 25 Routledge.

It serves a similar purpose to that which the English poet Shelley had claimed for poetry in *A Defence of Poetry* (1821):

Poetry lifts the veil from the hidden beauty of the world and makes familiar objects be as they were not familiar'   Shelley (1821) *In Defence of Poetry*

This of course poses the question of how does a material text transmute from a piece of everyday language or 'autotomised' experience in a piece of 'literature' this is what made this small group so radical. For there were suggesting that it lies in the formulaic devices within a text, rhythm, metaphor, image etc. That in turn lead to them being labelled in a derogatory manner 'Formalists', but it is also what underpins their perspective to a firm commitment to the material text. They tended towards understanding the materiality of the text as its primary importance and the literary devices which allowed this text to attain literariness which is consistent with a Materialist analysis derived from Marx and following Marxism the Russian Formalists comprehended 'texts' as being significant in the context of the social and economic period they were written in. However, they were clearly not 'Orthodox' literary Marxist scholars in the manner of Georg Lukács. Indeed, it is illuminating to examine the debate between Victor Shklovsky and Georg Lukács to inform the differences to the Formalist and this more 'orthodox' Marxist approach to literature. The orthodox approach to art is encapsulated by Plekhanov, the 'father of Russian Marxism':

As an adherent of the materialist conception of the world, I would say that the first task of the art critic is to translate the ideas of a work of art from the language of art into the the language of sociology, to establish what might be called the sociological equivalent of a given literary phenomenon.

See Plekhanov, G.V. (1955) Kunst and Literatur, Berlin And again by Lukács when he argues artistic concentration:

Is the maximum intensification in content of the *social?* and human essence of a given situation. Lukács, G (1978) Writer and Critic, London.

It is possible to perceive how the Formalists were concerned with the 'defamiliarization' or 'strangeness' of the individual literary text, what made it different and unique what they called its " literariness'; but literalness was critical for Lukács. For him the average person in the historical Realist novel was of the most significant as they 'reflected' authentic social relations and in all its contradictions. His criticism of Shklovsky and of the Formalists generally was scathing, for them:

The average character is nothing but an embodiment of uninspiring pedestrianism. Tihanov, G (2000) Victor Shklovsky and George Lukács in the 1930's. University College London.

So in conclusion to the question 'what is literature?'1) is it as Mathew Arnold, argued the quintessence of the 'best of humanity' transmogrified into a secular religion, 2) a special kind of writing which has the effect of 'defamiliarization' and therefore gives a text its literariness and allows the reader to see reality in a new light as the Russian Formalists maintained or 3) Georg Lukács' argument that it should represent everyday life and show its contradictions. I will leave the last words to Lenin:

One cannot life in society and be free of society. The freedom of the bourgeois writer is simply masked dependence on money.

We socialists expose this hypocrisy and rip off false labels, not in order to arrive at a non-class literature (that will only be possible in a socialist non-class society)...It will then be a free literature, become, the idea of socialism and sympathy with working people and not greed or careerism. .. 'Down with literary supermen! Literature must become *part* of the common cause of the proletariat, "cog and screw" of a greatialist mechanism set in motion by the entire vanguard of the the entire working class.'

Lenin. V. I. (1905) Party Organization and Party Literature, pp. 2-5. Moscow

William Trevor: 'The Story of Lucy Gault' in its socio-historical context.

Easter 1916.

> "………
>
> We know their dream, enough
> To know they dreamed and are dead;
> ………..
> Now and in time to be,
> Whenever green is worn,
> (they)
> Are changed, changed utterly,
> A terrible beauty is born."

-W.B.Yeats (1917)

This analysis will firstly explore a methodology in which to frame the William Trevor's novel, this will be a Marxist literary model, and, therefore, the text will be placed in its socio-political context: a process necessary for any meaningful critical analysis. Once the text is positioned in this context, it will be considered as an aspect in the development of the novel's plot. After this has been completed a critical analysis of p.187-190 will be constructed and, finally, some conclusions drawn.

A Marxist literary model would contest a statement such as "art for art's sake" because it perceives art and literature as being the products of the "dominant ideology", which in turn is produced by the current "mode of production" (Marx 1867); therefore under capitalism art and literature are, in the final analysis, inherently bourgeois. So, for Marxists, it is the tangible material conditions of an epoch which shape artistic products. The socioeconomic base determines the "relatively autonomous" superstructure of ideas.

Hence, when we examine Trevor's novel, it should be seen in the concrete conditions of the 'National Question' which dominated Irish society and culture in the 20th century, i.e. "the right of nations to self-determination" (Lenin 1916).

From this perspective, in regard to Trevor's novel, the insurrection in Dublin of Easter 1916, which was brutally suppressed by the British army, is of significance. Captain Gault was an ex-British army officer living in a country aflame with rebellion, the war of liberation only came to an end in late 1921. The abortive arson attack on his house would have been regarded by Fenians as "legitimate" revolutionary activity. It was this insurrectionary act which, ultimately, determines the course of the novel. The text of Trevor's novel can only be understood in the milieu in which it is acted out.

The text which will be examined (p 187-191) occurs at an important juncture in the plot, where themes of exile and return coalesce at Lahardane. Lucy's father has returned to Ireland and now Horahan revisits the house he attempted to destroy. Protestant and Catholic, bourgeoisie and the proletariat are placed in juxtaposition whilst Lucy is an observer, a lone actor on the stage of History. She is powerless as a solitary individual to influence events, this is Lucy's tragedy.

Horahan, speaking to Captain Gault, uses the language of Roman Catholic iconography with its emphasis on the cult of Mary. Mary is referred to by Catholics as "Our Lady". Horahan is committed to this discourse and, indeed,understands his salvation in these terms:

"It was Our Lady brought you back, sir".

- Trevor (2003).p 187.

Now Horahan can "confess" his sin, he is a "cripple for Ireland" (Trevor 2003).

Trevor has employed a play on words throughout the novel; Lucy's father refers to her as "Lady", a truncated version of "Our Lady". The Virgin Mary is believed, by Catholics, to have been conceived without sin, hence Lucy, as a child, was without "sin", but "time and circumstance" (Trevor 2003) have caused her demise and, indeed the downfall of her parents. A series of metaphors are employed to refine this position:

"The bees hover above the hives......the bees never stung her".

- ibid

Worker "bees" labour in harmony, but the storms of History can cause chaos, the metaphor is developed:

"....but once a wasp had been in her shoe".

- ibid

Bees are not predatory, the hive is an image used in the 20th century, (see Kollontai: 1923) to describe a society which was not, in its essence, alienated and divided. In contrast wasps exist outside of the hive and can be seen as a symbol for those who are estranged like Horahan.

Ireland in 1921 was experiencing massive contradictions; these are personified in the torment which Horahan experienced:

"(he was) struggling in his sleep against dreams which frightened him".

- ibid

Lucy is detached from the dialogue between her father and Horahan:

"She didn't know who Horahan was".

- Trevor (2003) p188.

And with an awful irony Lucy senses that Ralph may have returned:

"Would Ralph have set out? Would he have driven just a little way? Would this have accounted for the intensity of her intuition?"

- ibid

The repetition of questions is, here, a technique which has two functions:

1) To heighten the emotional significance of the situation.

2) Create pathos with Lucy because it is not, as she hoped, the man who loves her (Ralph) returning, but rather the man (Horahan) who was responsible for the concatenation of events which lead to Lucy's isolation.

The earthly "trinity" of men who have dominated her life: her father, Ralph and Horahan, have not brought the fruits of life that Lucy may have hoped for, but rather sadness and loneliness. This can be perceived as a condemnation of Patriarchy.

The device of Pathetic Fallacy is used to convey the Lucy's response to the meeting between her father and Horahan:

"A bird flapped against a window-pane, its wings beating in agitation before it recovered itself".

- Trevor (2003). p 189.

Lucy is this bird, denied access to the house (the hive), to the process of History and to the dialogues between men.

Finally the image of the crucified Christ with stigmata is used in regard of Horahan, the sacrifice of blood:

"The splinters savaged him when he knelt. Droplets of blood were warm on his legs.

- Trevor (2003). p 190.

But Horahan does not only suffer physically to achieve salvation, his Eucharistic sacrifice is also his sanity:

"She (Lucy) looked into the features of the man who had returned after so long and saw only madness".

- Trevor (2003). p 191.

Therefore the text and its context create the question: must Horahan have been mentally ill to have committed a revolutionary act in the context of Ireland

1921? It seems, to me, a mistake to confuse the two; not all Irish revolutionaries were "mad" or "bad", but were, rather the products of concrete socio-historical conditions of their historical epoch. It is Lucy's tragedy to be caught up in this bubbling cauldron as a child.

References.

Kollontai, A. (1923) *Love of Worker Bees*, Moscow: Progress Publishers.

Lenin, V.I. (1916) *The Socialist Revolution and The Right of Nations to Self-Determination*, Moscow: Progress Publishers.

Marx, K. (1887) in *Selected Works*, London: Lawrence and Wishart.

Trevor, W. (2003) *The Story of Lucy Gault*, London: Penguin Books.

Yeats, W.B. (1917) in *A New Selection*, London: Macmillan.

On creativity, excoricism and recovery

Creativity is a means of exorcising the ghosts that haunt your soul, torment your mind. The pen can do more than any priest or schaman.

> 'Many of the most sincere and gifted
>
> artists and writers in this capitalist world
>
> are conscious of a loss of reality.'
>
> - Ernst Fischer: 'The Necessity of Art'.

Some theorists of language, such as the 'Russian Formalists' have argued that this 'loss of reality' is a positive aspect to writing and the processes of language generally. The 'Formalists' existed before the revolution of October 1917 in Russia and thrived in the creativity of the post-revolutionary period of the 1920's, only to be crushed by the counter-revolutionary Stalinists during the 1930's. They moved attention away from the symbolist interpretation of literature to a more material approach to the text. What is of interest to us about them is the 'concept' of the 'defamaliarizating effect' or what they called 'making strange'. The first step of their argument is that literature is condensed by Jan Mukarosky:

> 'in the maximum of the foregrounding of the utterance, that is bring the act of expression to the foreground, into prominence for the reader.'
>
> - Mukarosky.

The concept of foregrounding therefore is to put the 'linguistic medium' i.e. literature at the front of our perceptions. Victor Shklovsky argues this creates estrangement or a defamaliarizating effect, by disrupting the everyday uses of language literature 'makes strange' the world of everyday life a and renews the readers lost capacity for a new experience; essentially literature disrupts the 'mundane' which is part of our experience of alienation under capitalism. Therefore it is possible to argue that a 'loss of reality' or even the process of 'making strange' can be understood as positive elements in writing.

Having established the idiosyncratic nature of 'authentic' writing I will now construct a model of consciousness and language as formed by Marx and Engels which will then be developed by the philosophy of language created by Valentin Voloshinov in the late 1920's. Then this model will be applied to the journey taken by Jean-Paul Sartre from his first novel of 1938: 'Nausea' which is a work of existential dread and horror which expresses the essence of Sartre's existentialism to his crowning philosophical text: 'Critique of Dialectical Reason' which offers a path to freedom through 'praxis' from the existential anguish of his early novel.

Firstly then how did Marx and Engels conceptualize and therefore understand the categories of and the relationship between consciousness and language? The response is multi-dimensional a) Marx to quote Terry Eagleton:

'Turned the whole history of philosophy of humanity on its head, revolutionized it with the statement: 'my method is movement upwards from the abstract to the concrete.'

- Eagleton.

This is the foundation for the overarching thesis I present here i.e. Historical and Dialectical Materialism. For Marx and Engels we live in a material world. b) The material source of consciousness is material:

'Thought and consciousness are products of the human brain.'

- Engels.

This may seem obvious, but for many people the source of awareness is not the brain but 'The Idea' (Hegel), a 'First Cause' (Aristotle) or a 'Supreme Being' (Thomas Aquinas). So what is the nature of this 'consciousness' described by Engels?

'First came labour; after it, and then side by side with it, articulate speech.'

- Engels.

This process is social and the result of people not only interacting with there environment but each other:

'in order to produce they enter into definite connections and relations with one another, and within these social connections and relations does their activity take place.'

- Marx.

Therefore labour and language are social in nature. This position is developed further:

'First labour, then articulate speech were the two main stimuli under the influence of which the brain of the ape gradually changed into the human brain. The development of labour brought the members of the community more closely together...these relations gave rise to the need for primitive man to speak and communicate with each other.'

- Schneierson.

Here, therefore, is the fundamental model on which this thesis is constructed upon. Now I will look at two models of language in the light of the model constructed above. First, Ferdinand de Saussure in his 'Course of General Linguistics'(1913) created a theory which would influence all following study of language. It consisted of a) There exists a pre-established or ahistorical structure of language before its realization as writing and speech.

b) It consisted of chains of 'signs'. Each 'sign' is made up of 1) Signifier which is the sound or written image of 2) the Signified or meaning/concept. e.g. in English the signifier 't r e e' is related to the signified Tree and therefore creates the word TREE. But this is random because in other languages the signified tree would have a different signifier...

Because for Saussure this structure is detached from socio-history it is profoundly opposed to Marxism, but a Russian Marxist linguist named Valentin Voloshinov took it up in a study called 'Marxism and the Study of Language' (1929). He accepted the concept of the 'sign':

'The entire reality of a word is absorbed in being a 'sign'.

- Voloshinov.

However ideology which here means both ideas and 'false consciousness' (Marx) is transmitted through language:

'everything ideological possesses semiotic (sign) value'.

- ibid.

So for Voloshinov the false dichotomy between the material base and ideological superstructure of classical Marxism is resolved through language or 'signs'. However he recognizes the limitations of the 'sign'

'Signs only arise...they become material only socially, they comprise a group and only then do they take (real) shape.'

-ibid.

But it is when 'sign' or words become what Saussure had called 'parole' or 'utterances' that they become significant i.e. both material and socially interactive. Language is as Engels had argued a defining human characteristic. Voloshinov enhances this position:

'In point of fact, the word is a two-sided act. It is determined equally by whose word it is and for whom it is meant.'

The 'word' therefore introduces not monologue but dialogue...we communicate with others, he concludes:

'A word is the product of the reciprocal relationship between speaker and listener. Each and every word the 'one in relation to the other"
- ibid.

I would now like to apply this theoretical construct to the journey taken by Jean-Paul Sartre from the existentialist 'dread' of his novel 'Nausea'(1938) to the concept of 'praxis' as a path to freedom in 'Critique of Dialectical Reason'(1960). A path through human creativity as social rather than merely individual which can be seen as the solution to 'absurdity' characterized as mental health issues. The central character in 'Nausea' says;

'The nausea has not left me, I think it will be some time before it does...it is no longer an illness or apassing fit: it is I.'

- Sartre (1938).

The words nausea or sickness appear in two other of Sartre's works; 1) 'The Psychology of the Imagination' (1940) 'are conscious of a nauseating sickness.' and 2) in his first major philosophical work 'Being and Nothingness' (1943) 'dullness...feeling of sickness.' Why? Sartre defines three modes of being a) 'Being-in-itself' this are objects which simply exist like a tree, b) 'Being-for-itself' this is humanity, because we have no pre-determined essence, there is no 'First Cause', for Sartre, we make ourselves, we create ourselves. It is the absurd contrast between these two forms of being which is one cause for Nausea, c)'Being-for-Others', here Sartre says we only become aware of our 'being' when in the 'gaze' of another, when someone 'looks' at you. Thus:

'I find myself in a state of instability in relation to the Other.'

- Sartre (1943).

This is where Sartre's infamous phrase 'Hell is other people' is derived from. Any belief in a system of ideas or faith was, according to Sartre at this time, 'bad faith'. But Sartre discovered the analytical tools provided by Marx and Engels and renewed them in order to explain and transcend this existential dread or 'Nausea' in 'Critique of Dialectical Reason': 1) he embraced Marx's concept of conscious human activity as the dynamic of History, once this was established he had to explain his early position of 'Nausea', 2) in order to achieve this Sartre created the idea of the 'Practico-inert' which is when humans are active but not social like atoms whirling around in a system and 3) he provided the solution of 'praxis' or 'depasssement' (going beyond the existing situation). This is a refinement of Marx's concept of 'species-being' which was, he said, the essence of humans i.e. to act interact with the world and each other. For Sartre 'praxis' and 'activity' are at the heart of the solution. This 'praxis' is genuine social activity created and made two-way by language:

'We set off from the immediate, that is to say the individual fulfilling him/herself to the totality of bonds with others...absolute concrete people.'

- Sartre (1960).

The social is creative and the creative is social, they are only divided in a social system which has what Marx called the 'division of labour' between mental and manual labour and ultimately between those who are compelled to sell 'social labour', which is their creativity, and to those who buy and profit from it. But the only way to prevent the commoditization of art is to abolish commodity capitalism; one is dependent on the other. But maintaining an active dialogue between artists and writers is a key step in breaking the chains of mental ill health and aiding recovery. Pick up you pen and write, and the chains of illness will dissolve.

On 20th century Irish poetry

This analysis examines the poetry of Heaney and Yeats within the context of 'The Irish Question' which dominated 20th century Irish poetry. The latter was summarized by Ralph Fox, as follows:

> For seven hundred years Ireland has been engaged in a struggle for national liberty... that of struggle for a free and independent Irish Workers' and Farmers' Republic.

> - Fox (1932), p 1.

I argue that resistance to British rule has informed modern Irish poetics, but that current of petty-bourgeois nationalism reflected in Irish poetry, although privileged by Lenin he also perceived as problematic. I show similarities, but also differentiate between Yeats and Heaney arguing they were 'legitimized' as 'cultural capital' by the Noble Prize. Finally I argue for an internationalist proletarian poetics and previllege Yeats.

Yeats as a young revolutionary Fenian and a spiritualist wrote prophetically in 1893 as the Twentieth Century dawned: *To Ireland in Coming Times*:

> Know, that I would accounted be

> True brother of a company

> That sang, to sweeten Ireland's wrong,

> -Yeats (2009) pp. 16-17.

He would controversially exclude Owen and other WW 1 poets from The Oxford Book of Modern Verse 1892-1935 in his *Introduction* (1936) on the basis that:

> ...passive suffering is not a theme for poetry.

> -Yeats (1936), section IX, pp xxi-xxii.

His rationale is apparent, but I see potential in Lenin *Leo Tolstoy and his Epoch* as literary method who was arguing that Tolstoy was 'an ideological *camera obscura*' (Eagleton+ Drew 2006, p. 42) of a pre-revolutionary society for a persuasive reading of Yeats and specifically Heaney *Punishment*:

> To identify the great artist with the revolution which he has obviously failed to understand, and from which he obviously stands aloof, may at first sight seem strange and artificial. A mirror which does not reflect things correctly could hardly be called a mirror... revolution, however, is an extremely complicated thing. ..Tolstoy's ideas are a mirror of the weakness, the short comings of our peasant revolt...Tolstoy reflected the pent-up hatred, the ripened striving for a better lot, the desire to get rid of the past.

-Lenin (1967) pp. 64-68

Lenin (1967) *Tolstoy and His Epoch* argued that great writers can describe complex pre-revolutionary circumstances up-side-down or camera obscura. Here Lenin made a major advance in modern aesthetics by showing that the dialectic, 'the unity of opposites' exists in literature is not merely as a straightforward reflection of reality. How is this pertinent to my discussion of Heaney and Yeats? I shall employ poetry by Bobby Sands to show the anti-imperialist poet 'telling' us what he believes and feels. However, Heaney and Yeats are closer to Tolstoy in context of Lenin's analysis in my reading. I shall illustrate this with Heaney's *Punishment*. Firstly I shall position the poem within Heaney's own narrative of his poetic development. In O'Driscoll (2009) *Stepping Stones: interviews with Seamus Heaney* Heaney was asked:

> Was the difficultly with *Punishment* more political than literary?

Heaney replied:

> That's not how I would put it, because that makes it sound as if I were 'addressing the situation in Northern Ireland'. Admittedly I 'addressed the situation' when I introduced different bog poems at readings...

What Anna Swir called 'the right to biological life' was the point and remains the point.

-O'Driscoll (2009) p. 159.

The narrative of the poem and the poem itself like many of Heaney's 'skinny quatrains' is ambivalent. They cannot be assessed by a Kantian aesthetic in the sense Copleston (1964) sums up as follows:

a) Disinterested interest.

b) Purposiveness without a concept of purpose.

c) Expression of feeling rather than a concept.

- Copleston (1964) vol six, part 11.

The imagery of *Punishment* Heaney (1998) pp 71-72) is derived from a dual narrative emanating from Heaney's reading of Glob (1969) *The Bog People: Iron-Age Man Preserved* and the 'punishment' beatings carried out or encouraged by the I.R.A. to enforce their ideological hegemony in Republican areas. Tarring and feathering was a method used mainly by Republican sympathizers rather than the I.R.A. Farrell, M (1976) and McCann, E (1974) give accounts of the structural causes and realities of conflict in the Northern Irish Statelet. Heaney *Punishment* continues:

> I can see her drowned body in the bog,

This references both the history of ancient sacrifices and undercurrent of 'land' for the Irish:

> her shaved head
>
> like a stubble of black corn,
>
> …
>
> Little adulteress,
>
> before they punished you

There is a suggestion of voyeurism here:

> who have stood dumb
>
> when your betraying sisters,
>
> cauled in tar,
>
> wept by the railings,

who would connive
in civilized outrage yet understand
the exact and tribal, intimate revenge.

-Heaney (1987) pp.

This is not the product of a writer of Tolstoy's stature, but exemplifies both the brutality and revolutionary zeal of the masses in a period of revolutionary turmoil, like Jacobean France or the North of Ireland after the smashing of the Civil Rights movement in Derry. It achieves a dialectical 'unity of opposites' in a world which is 'up-side-down'. Also note Heaney's, 'civilised outrage' which is almost a guilt response to 'intimate revenge' as Heaney had moved to the Republic in 1972.

Fox (1932) *Marx, Engels, Lenin on the Irish Revolution* introduced the revolutionary proletariat into Ireland's Zeitgeist. He maintained that Lenin understood the mass strike in Dublin during 1913 lead by James Larkin as a pivotal moment in Ireland:

Lenin emphasises that the Dublin strike, the organisation of the political party of the Irish workers, completely changed the situation in Ireland.

-Fox (1932) p. 12.

Hence we are able to perceive within the Marxian understanding of the Irish Question an anti-imperialist orientation with its suspicion of petty-bourgeois nationalism which manifest itself in Ireland in its most developed form as Fenianism. The Irish Marxist James Connelly argued 'only Marxism provides the clue to Irish history.' Fox (1932, p 28). Connelly was executed for leading the 'Citizens Army' during the 1916 Easter uprising. Lenin (1916) *Discussion on Self-Determination Summed-Up* commented ruefully on this insurrection:

It is the misfortune of the Irish that they rose prematurely, before the European revolt of the proletariat had had time to mature.

-Lenin (1964) p 364.

The sacrificial nature of the Mass is emblematic of the Easter Uprising and in comprehending a modern Irish poetics and because of this Yeats's *Easter 1916* reverberates through the century:

> Too long a sacrifice
>
> Can make a stone of the heart
>
> -Yeats (2009) pp 60-62.

These lines anticipated much as do:

> Was it needless death after all?
>
> For England may keep faith
>
> And what excess of love bewildered
>
> them till they died?
>
> I write it out in verse –
>
> MacDonald and MacBride
>
> And Connelly and Pearse
>
> Now and in time to be,
>
> Whenever green is worn,
>
> Are changed, changed utterly:
>
> A terrible beauty is born.
>
> - ibid

Yeats in *Easter 1916* uses both iambic tetrameter and iambic trimeter. The poem's rhyme scheme revolves around ABAB. The last line impacts, it is repeated three times in the poem, because 'terrible beauty' is an oxymoron and therefore it creates a sense of 'estrangement' as understood by the Russian Formalists. The final line employs alliteration of sounds **b**eauty/ **b**orn to effect and plays with notions of conception/revolution and beauty/terror.

To contrast, I now examine the writing of Bobby Sands composed while in the H-Blocks of Long Kesh prison (see Sands ([1983] 2001 *One Day in My Life* for a prose account of the brutal conditions endured by Republican prisoners). Sands *The Rhyme of Time* (1998, pp. 177-79) in which we may locate what Yeats *Easter*

1916 (Yeats 2009, p 62) called 'terrible beauty'. The last stanza of Bobby Sands' poem, after describing the struggles of the oppressed across the world throughout history, concludes:

> It lights the darkness of this prison cell,
>
> It thunders forth its might,
>
> It is "the indistinguishable thought,"
>
> my friend,
>
> The thought that says "I'm right!"

-Sands (1998) p 179.

This is instrumentalist poetry, but tempered by concluding with the first-person speaker, we are given access to Sands psyche. Sands show how the certitude and single-mindedness of the anti-imperialist urban guerrilla almost shouts at his oppressor with the rhyme of 'might/right'. The anaphora of 'It' either inspires or intimidates the addressee. And the final trimeter ends after two iambic feet with the emphatic and gun steeled spondee 'I'm right!' As Frantz Fanon (1965) had noted:

> The native intellectual who takes up arms to defend his nation's legitimacy, who is willing to strip himself naked to study the history of his body, is obliged to dissect the heart of his people.

-Fanon (1965), p 211.

For the Orthodox Marxist the Irish Question and its literature are contradictory because its petty-bourgeois nationalism is incapable of casting off the shackles of imperial domination and creating socialism. These concrete and contradictory forces, I argue, formed both the poetry of Yeats and Heaney providing an explanation for their similarities and differences and their ultimate failure to provide a poetics of Irish liberation (indeed neither did Sands). So we can read Auden ([1940] 1985) *In Memory of W.B. Yeats* in a similar ideological fashion to Ralph Fox (1932), they both went to Spain with the International Brigades, Fox died. In his poem upon the death W.B.Yeats Auden makes a Marxian ideological as well as aesthetic point on the limitations of Irish nationalism and poetry to change society:

> Mad Ireland hurt you into poetry.
>
> Now Ireland has her madness and
>
> her weather still,
>
> For *poetry makes nothing happen*[10]: it survives
>
> -Auden (1981) pp.141-3.

Here is Heaney's response to Auden's position on Yeats in the early 1970's:

> I am tired of speculations about the relation of the poet's work to the workings of the world he inhabits, and finally I disagree that *'poetry makes nothing happen.'*[11] It can eventually make new feelings, or feelings about feelings happen, and anybody can see that in this country for a long time to come a refinement of feelings will be more urgent than a reframing of policies or of constitutions.
>
> -O'Donoghue (2009) p 6.

I argue that Yeats *Easter 1916* (2009, p.62) 'I wrote it out in verse.' and Heaney *Digging* (1985 p. 2):

> Between my finger and thumb
>
> The squat gun rests, snug as a pen.
>
> I'll dig with it.
>
> -Heaney (1987) p 2.

Unlike Owen they were absent. Yeats, whose class orientation was from the Protestant Ascendency embraced Republicanism and occultism and Heaney was a privelliged working class Catholic poet. They both in the first-person singular and within the Irish nationalist poetic narrative 'aestheticize' (Brown, 2005, p. 26, 8) violence and do so from distance unlike Sands.

---

[10] My Italics
[11] My italics.

'Poetry is as unfair as history. Seamus Heaney takes his distances –…but his Derry is always with him.'

- Gupta and Johnston (2005) p 264.

Yeats, Eagleton argues, engage with politics but did so with a 'Romantic inspirationalism and irrationalism'. We can understand Years in 'an aesthetic of visionary spontaneity' rather like William Blake (Eagleton pp 102 -3) while Heaney's 'art is about craft and production (ibid).

Lenin (1979) *The Right of Nations to Self-Determination* privileges the oppressed:

Insofar as the bourgeoisie of the oppressed nation fights the oppressor, we are always, in every case, and more in favour, we are the most consistent enemies of oppression.

-Lenin (1979) p 23.

Modern Irish poetics was formed by nationalist discontent but flourished in difficult circumstances. Brecht encapsulates this enigma:

In the dark times

Will there also be singing?

Yes, there will also be singing.

About the dark times.

-Brecht (1976) p.320.

James Connelly maintained:

The Irish working class must emancipate itself, and in emancipating itself free its own country.

-Bambery (1986) p.26.

Therefore, only the proletariat can bring about the national and linguistic liberation which Irish poetry required. Yeats and Heaney as Noble Prize laureates were legitimized as 'cultural capital.' (Bourdieu, 1984, p 17). However, finally like Edward Said I favour Yeats:

Yeats stopped short of imagining the full political liberation he might have aspired toward, but we are left with a considerable achievement in decolonization nonetheless.

-Said (1988) p 65.

Bibliography.

Auden, W, H (1981) *Collected Shorter Poems 1927-1957*, London: Faber & Faber.

Bambery, C (1986) *Ireland's Permanent Revolution*, London, Bookmarks

Bourdieu, P. ({1979] 1984) *Distinction: A Social Critique of the Judgement of Taste*, trans, by R. Nice, London: Routledge.

Brecht, B (1976) *Poems 1913-1956*, London: Eyre Methuen Ltd.

Danson Brown, R The poetry of Seamus Heaney, *The Popular & The Canonical, Debating 20th Century Literature 1940-2000*, Milton Keynes: The Oxford University.

Copleston, F (1964) *A History of Philosophy: Volume Six, Modern Philosophy; Part II, Kant,* New York: Image Books.

Eagleton, T (1980) Review of Field Work *New Casebooks* (ed) Allen, M *Seamus Heaney Contemporary Critical Essays*, Basingstoke Hampshire, Palgrave MacMillan

Eagleton & Drew (2006) *Marxist Literary Theory*, Oxford, Blackwell Publishing.

Fanon, F (1965) *The Wretched of the Earth*, New York: Grove Press.

Farrell, M (1976) *Northern Ireland: The Orange State*, London: Plato Press.

Fox, R (1932) *Marx, Engels, Lenin on the Irish Revolution*, London: Modern Books.

Glob, P.V (1969) *The Bog People: Iron-Age Man Preserved*, London: Faber & Faber.

Gupta & Johnston (2005) *A Twentieth-Century Reader, Texts and Debates*, Milton Keynes: The Open University

Heaney, S (1987) *New Selected Poems 1966-1987*, London: Faber & Faber.

Lenin. V. I (1964) *Collected Works vol 22*, Moscow: Progress Publishers.

Lenin, V. I (1967) *On Art and Literature*, Moscow: Progress Publishers.

Lenin V. I (1979) *On the Rights of Nations to Self-Determination,* Moscow: Progress Publishers.

Longley, E (1985) *'North'* "Inner Émigré" or "Artful Voyeur" in T. Curtis (ed), *The art of Seamus Heaney*, Bridgend: Poetry Wales, Dufor Editions.

McCann, E (1974) *War in an Irish Town*, London: Penguin Books.

O'Donoghue (2008) *The Cambridge Companion to Seamus Heaney*, Cambridge: Cambridge University Press.

O'Driscoll, D (2009) *Stepping Stones: interviews with Seamus Heaney*, London: Faber & Faber.

Said, E (1988) *Yeats and Decolonization* in Eagleton (ed). Nationalism, Colonialism, and Literature, University Press of Minnesota - A. Kindle Edition.

Sands, B ([1983] 2001) *A Day in my Life*, Cork: Mercer Press.

Sands, B (1998) *Writings from Prison*, Cork: Mercier Press

Yeats, W.B (2009) *W.B.Yeats Poems*, London: Faber & Faber.

Yeats. W.B. (1936) *Introduction to* The Oxford Book of Modern Verse 1892-1935, Oxford: Clarendon.

Red Rebel.

Vladimir Mayakovsky was a great poet who challenged the conventions both in the world of poetry and in the social sphere. For many of those of us who see the workers revolution in Russia of October 1917 as the pinnacle of human endeavour and within its theory the foundations for the future human attainment it, therefore, follows that as the most significant poet of the Russian insurrectionary masses of October 1917 Mayakovsky represents the highest level of achievement in modern poetry. Leon Trotsky wrote in his study of revolutionary writing, 'Literature and Revolution' that proletarian poets like Mayakovsky:

Have to) reshape the world of feelings. Not everybody is capable of it. That is why there are many people in this world that think as revolutionaries and feel as Philistines

- Leon Trotsky.

His artistic talents were not, however, confined to poetry, he designed book coversss well as Agitprop posters and, also drew .

Mayakovsky was born in Russia in 1893. After the premature death of his father the family moved to Moscow, here his elder sister Lyudmila became a student and was radicalized by Marxists. She brought home socialist literature, both legal and illegal and Vladimir was set on fire, intellectually and emotionally, by this material. At the age of 14 he joined the Bolshevik Party. In 1908 he was arrested for possession of revolutionary proclamations, he was placed on probation. Later during the same year Mayakovsky was enrolled in the Moscow Art School, it was while a student there that he became aware of the Futurist movement. Vladimir was arrested again in 1909 for political activism. A report written by one of the wardens confirmed his revolutionary credentials:

Vladimir Mayakovsky by his behavior incites the other prisoners to disobedience towards prison wardens.......purporting to be the prisoners spokesman.

He was moved around the prison system and eventually placed in solitary confinement; it was whilst in "solitary" that he wrote his first poem. By 1912 Mayakovsky was out of prison and in the December of that year published a Futurist Manifesto called: 'A Slap in the Face of Public Taste', this is reproduced below:

 A Slap in the Face of Public Taste

To the readers of our New First Unexpected.

We alone were the face of our Time. Through us the horn of time blows in the art of the world.

The past is too tight. The Academy and Pushkin are less intelligible than hieroglyphics.

Throw Pushkin, Dostoevsky, Tolstoy, etc., etc. overboard from the Ship of Modernity.

He who does not forget his first love will not recognize his last.

Who, trustingly, would turn his last love toward Balmont's perfumed lechery? Is this the reflection of today's virile soul?

Who, faint-heartedly, would fear tearing from warrior Bryusov's black tuxedo the paper armor-plate? Or does the dawn of unknown beauties shine from it?

Wash your hands which have touched the filthy slime of the books written by the countless Leonid Andreyevs.

All those Maxim Gorkys, Krupins, Bloks, Sologubs, Remizovs, Averchenkos, Chornys, Kuzmins, Bunins, etc. need only a dacha on the river. Such is the reward fate gives tailors.

From the heights of skyscrapers we gaze at their insignificance!

We order that the poets' rights be revered:

- To enlarge the scope of the poet's vocabulary with arbitrary and derivative words (Word-novelty).

- To feel an insurmountable hatred for the language existing before their time.

- To push with horror off their proud brow the Wreath of cheap fame that You have made from bathhouse switches.

- To stand on the rock of the word "we" amidst the sea of boos and outrage.

And if for the time being the filthy stigmas of your "common sense" and "good taste" are still present in our lines, these same lines for the first time already glimmer with the Summer Lightning of the New Coming Beauty of the Self-sufficient (self-centered) Word.

David Burliuk, Alexander Kruchenykh, Vladmir Mayakovsky, Victor Khlebnikov

Their manifesto was an outcry against the literary establishment, a celebration of the new in art and poetry and an attack on so-called common sense. Russian Futurism was opposed to all forms of deification whether by the Romantic poets of Nature or any other form of mysticism. They believed in breaking the mould and saw in the rhythms of the machine and the throbbing of the oppressed masses a new style for both poetry and society. Essentially Mayakovsky and his fellow poets and artists believed in removing the artificial boundary between art and everyday life which had been created by the bourgeois culture. They would travel around Russia and perform spontaneous shows of poetry, drama and art in the way that would be repeated during the1960's, when another movement of radical ideas in the arena of art and politics would arise; these impromptu art events were called "happenings". Also in 1912 his first poems were published.

By 1914 the old political radicalism had returned to Mayakovsky and because of this he was expelled from the Moscow Art School. That year his first long poem: 'A Cloud in Trousers' was published, it is very significant because of the combination of its themes of revolution, love art and religion from the perspective of a rejected lover. However its most important contribution to modern literature is that Mayakovsky used the language of the street:

> "Your thoughts,
>
> dreaming on a softened brain,
>
> like an over-fed lackey on a greasy settee,
>
> with my heart's bloody tatters I'll mock again;
>
> impudent and caustic, I'll jeer to superfluity.
>
> Of Grandfatherly gentleness I'm devoid,
>
> there's not a single grey hair in my soul!
>
> Thundering the world with the might of my voice,
>
> I go by -- handsome,
>
> twenty-two-year-old.
>
> If you like-
>
> I'll be furiously flesh elemental,
>
> or - changing to tones that the sunset arouses
>
> if you like-
>
> I'll be extraordinary gentle,
>
> not a man, but - a cloud in trousers!"

(He continues arguing that the poverty-stricken and labour exhausted outcasts will slowly become aware of their moral superiority over the corrupt and decaying capitalist world):

> "I know, the sun would fade out, almost,
>
> stunned by our souls Hellenic beauty".
>
> - Mayakovsky.

In the summer of 1915 Mayakovsky fell in love, it was to be the greatest love of his life, with Lilya Birk. She was married to Osip Brik who was his publisher, but despite her marriage Lilya fell in love with Mayakovsky.

Lilya and Vladimir. Describing the evening they met Osip Brik said:

"His reading was fascinating. It was what we had been waiting for. We had not been able to read anything for some time. All poetry seemed worthless-- poets were writing not in the right way and not about the right things, and here suddenly was both.

When she told her husband that she'd fallen in love:

"all three of us decided never to part from one another."

- Lilya Birk.

The Russian proletariat led by the Bolshevik Party seized power in the revolution of October 1917, this was only the second time the working class had overthrown the class oppression of capitalism, the other being the 'Paris Commune' of 1871. This revolt was the pivotal point in world History which is the History of class struggle and heralded in a new epoch for humanity. Lenin had maintained that in these circumstances:

"(poets and artists) are the cogs and wheels of the whole revolutionary machine."

- Lenin.

Mayakovsky was at the heart of the insurrection; indeed as 'Red' sailors stormed the 'Winter Palace' they chanted one of his slogans:

"Eat peaches, chew on quail

Your last day is coming, bourgeois!"

As the struggle to maintain and spread the revolution intensified Mayakovsky contuned to write some of his best know poems.

However, this poem from 1914 provides the reader with an understanding of the depths within

Mayakovsky as a crafter of poetry:

Listen!
Listen,
if stars are lit
it means - there is someone who needs it.
It means - someone wants them to be,
that someone deems those specks of spit
magnificent.

And overwrought,
in the swirls of afternoon dust,
he bursts in on God,
afraid he might be already late.
In tears,
he kisses God's sinewy hand
and begs him to guarantee
that there will definitely be a star.
He swears
he won't be able to stand
that starless ordeal.

Later,
He wanders around, worried,
but outwardly calm.

And to everyone else, he says:
'Now,
it's all right.
You are no longer afraid,
are you?'

Listen,
if stars are lit,
it means - there is someone who needs it.
It means it is essential
that every evening
at least one star should ascend
over the crest of the building.
                    - Mayakovsky.

The link between the aesthetic and the bohemian revolt of the leftist Futurists and the revolutionary Marxist poet-revolutionaries is clear. Mayakovsky and his circle were from a disaffected and an untamed segment of the left intelligentsia which refused to be incorporated into the bourgeoisie and, therefore, into capitalism. In other words they didn't "sell-out". Their orientation could, hence, only be towards the exploited and downtrodden masses and the role of leading them in a revolutionary struggle. Mayakovsky's development as a human being, a poet and a revolutionary, was therefore profoundly connected to the fate of the Russian Revolution. The years 1922-1928 saw him as a leading member of the 'Left Art Front' which was active in spreading the revolution. At this time he was defining his work as "Communist Futurism". As the betrayal of the revolution by the Stalinist reactionaries that took place after the death of Lenin, this had its material foundations in the inability of the 'Union of Soviet Socialist Republics' (the Workers State) to spread its revolution internationally, the gains of the 1917 revolution were being rolled back. As a result Mayakovsky began to decline artistically and emotionally. He was being constrained by a system which had heralded the dawn of human freedom, but was now acting against the interests of the masses. In 1929 he was compelled to join the bureaucratically controlled 'Soviet Association of Proletarian Poets'. The same year he fell in love with Tatiana Yakovleva, but sadly this relationship wasn't to be successful. The failure of the revolution combined with sadness in love was too much for him, on the evening of April 14th 1930 Mayakovsky committed suicide by shooting himself. There is some evidence that he had played 'Russian Roulette' [placing a revolver to his head with one bullet in six chambers and pulling the trigger one or twice]. He eloquently describes his inner contradictions:

'On the Top of my Voice'.

Agitprop sticks in my teeth too,

and I'd rather compose romances for you--

more profit in it and more charm

But I subdued myself,

setting my heel on the throat

of my own song.

Listen, comrades of prosperity,

to the agitator, the rabble-rouser.

Stifling the torrents of poetry,

I'll skip the volumes of lyrics;

as one alive, I'll address the living.

I'll join you in the far communist future.

- Mayakovsky

In an analysis of progressive writers the Marxist thinker Leon Trotsky said:

"The poetry of Mayakovsky was more bohemian than proletarian".

-Trotsky.

I will leave the last words with the great proletarian Bard himself, an excellent poem in my view:

Shallow philosophy on deep waters

Gonna turn if not into Tolstoy,

then into a fat sea-buoy –

eat, write, heat-stricken.

Who hasn't philosophized on deep waters?

Waters.

Yesterday,

the ocean was wickedly fierce.

Today,

it is meeker

than dove hatching.
So what!
All things disperse …
All things are changing.

There's an order
in ocean waters:
Ebb,
or flow.
While Steklov's pen
has constant waters
In defiance of a law.

Dead fish
swim alone.
Flippers hang like they're broken.
It swims
for weeks,
And don't care
if it's got any token.

Opposite us,
slower than a seal,
A steamer from Mexico,
While we sail thither.
Can't be different.
Labour division.

This is a whale, - they say.
Could be.
Like our fishy Bedny – not thin.

Only, Damian has moustaches looking
outward,
While the whale's -
Within.

Years – sea gulls.
Rush in the sky –
And - hurtle in waters -
to feed their bellies.
No more seagulls.
Actually,
Where are the birdies ?

I was born,
grown,
fed with a comforter,
Worked,
become worn-out…
Here's how life would pass
as we've just passed
the Asore Islands.

       -Mayakovsky.

Towards a literature of liberation.

What is meant by the word "creative"? How has the nature of this concept developed since the ancient Greeks? How are we to explain the "absurdist" tendency in modern literature? This thesis will argue that, essentially, art is a reflection of given socio-economic conditions into the sphere of ideas, that literature is the highest form of human endeavour, but the creative aspirations of humanity can only achieve fulfilment when the material basis of society is transformed by the seizure of the "means of production" by the oppressed and the, consequent, socialisation of everyday life.

The word "creative" can be traced back to the Renaissance, however these thinkers were profoundly influenced by ancient Greeks such as Aristotle and Plato. his translation of the Greek word for creativity "mimesis" is "doing what another has done." "or making something like something else." Hence Aristotle wrote of the process of "mimesis":

> "The general origin of poetry was due to two causes, each of them part of human nature, firstly that s/he is the most imitative creature in the world and secondly, that human being delights in works of imitation."

-Aristotle: Poetics.

For Aristotle the poet imitates the "real" and therefore gives meaning to that object. He expands his ideas:

> "The poet's function is to describe, not something that has happened, but a kind of thing that might happen."

- Aristotle: Poetics.

Hence although poetry is rooted in the real it transcends this condition.

Plato regards the artist, also, as an "imitator", but twice removed from the source. Firstly, from the "Idea"

(Divinity) who s/he imitates and secondly from the workman who produces things for the artist to imitate. Plato believed that poetry was a deviation from the "Idea" or "Reason" and it therefore:

> "Excites and feeds this worthless part of the soul and thus destroys the rational part."

-Plato: Republic.

However, he concluded that as the "Idea" or "Reason" is the source of all things and as the poet describes reality, he must be divinely inspired.

These ideas had a profound influence during the Renaissance. Four significant areas of art theory arose in this epoch:

5) Art was seen to be a imitation of a hidden reality, this concept was employed by some Christian thinkers who argued that art was a reflection of the Divine.

6) Art can be seen as emanating from an esoteric reality which was seen as a reflection of the "Idea of Beauty."

7) In a similar vein art was perceived as the "idealisation of Nature."

8) Finally the concept of the creative is seen as being the product of a split between nature and humanity.

These, and similar ideas, lead some writers to conclude:

> "There are two creators, God and the poet."

- Tasso (1544-95).

But ideas do not develop, as theorists such as Hegel maintained, like an abstract process moving through history. Hegel separated ideas from their human subject, however Marx formed a critique of his position and developed a materialist philosophy in opposition to this theory of abstractions:

"(humanity) lives with eyes and ears, living in the world, in Nature."

- Karl Marx: Economic and Philosophical Manuscripts.

The foundation for a materialist conception of art is forming here. Human activity is not passive, we interact with nature in order to transform it through " practical sensuous activity"(Karl Marx: Thesis on Feuerbach). Therefore we are beings who engage with nature in an attempt to develop it, but we are also social beings and our awareness is formed by social experience:

"What is going on in our minds has always been, and will always be a product of society."

-Karl Marx: Grundrisse.

However this essay dose not wish to construct what can be called a "vulgar reflectionist" theory of literature. Art is more complex than this, as Bertolt Brecht, the German poet and playwright, put it:

"Art reflects with special mirrors."

- Brecht: The Popular and the Realistic.

These mirrors should not be passive reflections of a society founded on commodity production i.e. where our labour is wrenched from us by capitalists and as a consequence appears as an "alien object" (Marx) to ourselves and to fellow workers. Artists and poets can, as Brecht argued, challenge the continuing "passivisation" of culture in the modern epoch. One method of developing this resistance is to embrace an avant-guard art which provides, within itself, the spark of a new dawn. The avant-guard movement made statements such as:

"It is not me who is the clown, but this monstrously cynical society."

- Salvador Dali.

But this movement of poets and artists, which is revolutionary in nature, must, as Mao Tse-tung reflected, be rooted in the oppressed and disaffected:

> "Artists and writers should work in their own fields, which are art and literature,
>
> but their duty first and foremost is to understand and know the people well. Otherwise, for all your labour, you will have nothing to work on and will become empty-headed artists or writers."

> - Mao Tse-tung: Selected Works, vol. 4.

Therefore the most progressive currents are the avant-grade and the "socialist realist" movements. However what happens when these two tendencies are not bound in solidarity? It is instructive to examine the "absurdists" in this context, particularly the work of Franz Kafka:

> "Franz Kafka is the classic example of the

modern writer at the mercy of panic-stricken angst."

> -George Lukas: The Meaning of Contemporary Realism.

Kafka expresses this "angst" in his novel, 'The Trial'. Its major character, Joseph K., is confronted by an atomised society where social relations are clad in absurdity and there is a domineering and anonymous state. He is accused of a crime which is not defined and his trial is a farce. This is a manifestation of a disintegrating capitalism where solace is not found in social interaction, which is commodified, and there is also the nightmare of an oppressive state apparatus. In his short story, 'Metamorphosis' a person turns into a beetle and is rejected by both society and the family. This is a society where existential crisis is the norm and nothingness the refuge: capitalism in decline without a solution.

A poem by D.H Lawrence seems, to me, to wed the themes of an Avant-grade movement with a revolutionary aspiration:

A Sane Revolution.

If you make a revolution , make it for fun,

don't make it in ghastly seriousness,

don't do it in deadly earnest,

do it for fun.

Don't do it for international Labour.

Labour is the one thing a man has had too much of.

Let's abolish labour, let's have done with labouring!

Work can be fun, and men can enjoy it; then it's not labour.

Let's have it so! Let's make a revolution for fun.

-D.H.Lawrence: Selected Works.

Revolutions are made for 'fun' though, to quote Marx 'they are the locomotives of History'. So in the circumstances of communism in a post- revolutionary situation:

"The average human type will rise to the heights of an Aristotle, a Goethe, or a Marx."

-Leon Trotsky: Literature and Revolution.

"Be realistic, demand the impossible."

Situationalist graffiti in Paris during the revolution of 1968. On the nature of economic crisis: a Marxist defence.

Unless capitalism is an inherently crisis ridden system, Marxian socialists have their raison d'être removed. Marx himself recognized this when he maintained 'the law of the tendency of the rate of profit to fall' is:

In every respect the most important law of modern political economy.

-Marx (1973) *Capital vol 3*, p748.

And of the many causes of the economic crisis, underconsumptionism, financial bubbles Marx thought 'the law of the tendency of the rate of profit to fall' was the key to understanding that in the last instant capitalism must create the conditions for its own demise. This theory is amongst economists known as T.R.P.F and it is controversial even within schools of Marxist thought. This controversy has raged almost since the publication first appeared in print of *Volume Three of Capital* in 1894.

> The argument was and is important. For Marx's theory leads to the conclusion that the there is a fundamental, unreformable flaw in capitalism. The rate of profit is the key to capitalists being able to achieve their goal of accumulation. But the more accumulation takes place, the more difficult it is for them make sufficient profit to sustain it.
>
> -Harman (2007)*The rate of profit and the world today*

The lack of pristine clarity in Marx's writing has led to some confusion and is as Alex Callinicos (2014) *Deciphering Capital* argue partly an epistemological problem. Marx died in 1883 leaving only *Volume One of Capital* in print and his other manuscripts disordered. His lifelong friend Fredrick Engels and his daughter Eleanor Marx put together volumes two and three of *Capital* and the German Marxist intellectual Karl Kauksky the final volume sometimes knows as *Theories of Surplus Value*. Unfortunately, Marx had died before he completed his last and possibly most important componant of the project: ' the book of crisis' Callinicos (20114 p. 57) Alex Callinicos also argues in (2014) *Deciphering Capital* that the present crisis was caused by a combination of T.R.P.F, and a 'financial bubble'. So with these collieries in place I shall not only delineate the foundations of T.R.P.F itself but examine the argument. I shall conclude that capitalism does contain the germ of its own destruction within its very nature, but that this is not mere economic determinism and to this end quote Leon Trotsky:

> 'The proletariat grows and strengthens together with the growth of capitalism… But the day and hour power passes into the hands of the proletariat depend not directly upon the state of the productive forces, but upon the condition of the class struggle, upon the international situation, finally on subjective forces; tradition, initiative, readiness for struggle…'
>
> -Cliff (2000*) Marxism at the Millennium*, p. 38.

So we have an economic law that indicates a societal change, but this does not translate mechanistically into social transformation at a given time and place.

However, it is necessary to put in place some fundamental building blocks of Marxist political economy before we can continue. Firstly the 'labour theory of value' argues that it is 'living labour' that creates goods under capitalism, which are 'use-values, but because of the historically specific and unique nature of capitalism, they become not only 'exchange-values', but commodities, this is peculiar to the social-historical period of humanity's development we call capitalism, Marx argued. It is neither natural nor immutable, quite the opposite it has produced its own 'gravediggers' in the blue and white collar working class. Firstly, let me put some important methodology in place:

> In the social production of their existence, men inevitably enter into definite relations, which are independent of their will, namely relations of production appropriate to a given stage in the development of their material forces of production. The totality of these relations of production constitutes the economic structure of society, the real foundation, on which arises a legal and

political superstructure and to which correspond definite forms of social consciousness.

-Marx (1977) *Early Writings*, p. 425

Therefore, we make our own history, but the circumstances in which we do are not of our choosing, to paraphrase Marx. The commodity nature of Capitalism is delineated on the very first page of Capital Vol. 1:

> The wealth of those societies in which the capitalist mode of production prevails, presents itself as "an immense accumulation of commodities," its unit being a single commodity. Our investigation must therefore begin with the analysis of a commodity.

-Marx (1974) *Capital Vol 1*, p. 1.

So what does a commodity consist of? The investors' money, NO, although as we shall see that is a component. A simple commodity is made up of 'living labour' and 'dead labour', it is the activity of the 'living labour', the foundry worker the call-centre worker that creates the value. Money does not grow on trees, commodities are made and exchanged for money thus: C-M-C, the commodity does not create the money nor the money the commodity, so what does: 'living labour', the amount of 'socially necessary labour time' that the workers put in to create a good'. 'Socially necessary labour time is here explained by Choonara (2009) *Unravelling Capitalism:*

> There is an obviously objection to Marx's theory, not everyone works as hard."Socially necessary labour time' is the labour time needed by a society to produce a commodity with the average degree of skill and intensity prevalent at that time'. It creates a world in which all artistry is removed from work by the application of machinery and the divisions

of labour.' [e.g Between mental and physical work].

-Choonara (2009) *Unravelling Capitalism*, pp. 22-23.

It was Marx's concept of 'socially necessary labour time' that differentiated from and developed David Riccardo's initial 'labour theory of value' which was based on rents and land. Also Marx didn't spurn Adam Smith's concept of the importance of supply and demand, although he didn't agree with Smith 'hidden hand' or 'price equilibrium'. Both Smith and Ricardo, although significant, were limited by comparison with Marx.

So, what is the difference between 'living labour' and 'dead labour'. Another way of expressing these are as 'value': 'variable value' is living labour, the workers and 'constant value' is the machinery, computers, infrastructure etc. We have established where 'value' emanates from 'labour', but what about profit. To use a simple example, suppose a printer produces a 10 books a day, each book has a value of fifty pence $10 \times 50p = £5$. However, the worker is only paid for 60% of her or his labour as a wage £3 the other 40%, although created by the printer, is siphoned off into 'Surplus Value' which the capitalist will then translate into money= profit. We can see he worker is swindled out of £2 per day, which is generalised to create a rate of profit. This is the dark heart of capitalism, you may think you are doing a fair day's work for a fair day's pay, but you are being exploited in the essence of your being, your work. This can be articulated as an abstraction: humans interact with the Nature in order to transform Nature, and in this process transform themselves, this is what the young Marx called humanity's *species being*. As the product of your labour is not your's or your class' but is expropriated by the capitalist, the worker can be seen to be *estranged* from their work, from their essence. So even in relatively high paid jobs the work is inherently dehumanizing under capitalism. Marx encapsulated his theory of alienation, thus:

> The worker places his life in the object; but now it now longer belongs to him

-Marx (1977) Early Writings, p. 324.

There is another axis in capitalism as well as worker/capitalist one and that is that capitalists are compelled to compete with each other to generate profits to reinvest, to generate profits etc., 'accumulation for accumulation's sake.'(Marx).

The anarchy of the market, the ravaging of Nature without sustainability, the 'economics of the madhouse' to quote Chris Harman. There is a consequence for the capitalist of this though he must reinvest in 'dead labour', 'constant capital' in the insane completion with other capitalists. This creates a relationship which Marx called the 'organic composition of capital'. Which he describes in this way:

> The composition of capital is to be understood in a twofold sense. On the side of value, it is determined by the proportion in which it is divided into constant capital or value of the means of production, and variable capital or value of labour power, the sum total of wages. On the side of material, as it functions in the process of production, all capital is divided into means of production and living labour power. This latter composition is determined by the relation between the mass of the means of production employed, on the one hand, and the mass of labour necessary for their employment on the other. I call the former the value-composition, the atter the technical composition of capital.Between the two there is a strict correlation. To express this, I call the value composition of capital, in so far as it is determined by its technical composition and mirrors the changes of the

> latter, the organic composition of capital. Wherever I refer to the composition of capital, without further qualification, its organic composition is always understood.

> -Marx (1974) *Capital Vol 1,* p 574.

Therefore the capitalist must invest 'constant capital', dead labour' which has the consequence that Marx points out:

> The rate of self expansion of capitalism, or the rate of profit, being the goal of capitalist production, its fall...appears as a threat to the capitalist production process...This "testifies to the merely historical, transitory character of the capitalist mode of production" and the way that "at a certain stage it conflicts with its own further development". It showed that "the real barrier of capitalist production was capital itself.

So the demise of capitalism is an inherent aspect of itself. So why is it still here. Trotsky quoted above in a part of the answer. However to correct this overproduction of dead labour, machines, etc. Capitalism must decapitalize or devalue some capital. We are now beginning to examine what Marx called the 'countervailing tendencies':

1) Export of capital, 2) expansion of share capital, 3) extension of credit, 4) reduction of the value of labour power, 5) reduction of the value of constant capital, 6) spending on arms production, waste. The problem of capitalism is that although they may solve the problem in the short-term, they exacerbate it to the point of global destruction in the long run. .

There are essentially two schools of thought amongst orthodox Marxists a) Some have argued that the rate of profit will tend to decline in the long term, there will be booms and slumps, but there will be a long term downward trend, making each boom shorter than the one before and each slump deeper. b) Others Marxists believe that the devaluing of capital restore the rate of profit to its earlier level, these Marxists see intense crises of restructuring, not an inevitable long term decline. The former is closer to reality, but I also contend that capitalism transforms itself into different modes. We can see some clear epochs a) Classical Capitalism, b) The birth of Imperialism, c) 1930's recession and the growth of State Capitalism, d) the long boom and the 'permanent arms economy', e) the present crisis.

We can say for certain the crises will reoccur, as Chris Harman argued:

> What matters is to recognise that the system has only been able to survive—and even, spasmodically, grow quite fast for the past three decades—because of its recurrent crises, the increased pressure on workers' conditions and the vast amounts of potential inevitable value that are diverted into waste. It has not been able to return to the "golden age" and it will not be able to do so in future. It may not be in permanent crisis, but it is in a phase of repeated crises from which it cannot escape, and these will necessarily be political and social as well as economic.
>
> -Harman (2007) *The rate of profit and the world today.*

In other words, there is nothing inevitable about the success of the socialist revolution, but there is about the probability for the conditions of such a revolution to be created paradoxically by the inherent tendencies of capitalism. There has been a recession since Harman wrote '*The rate of profit and the world today*' and now to quote Trotsky:

> The economic prerequisite for the proletarian revolution has been achieved...the task of the next period...consists in overcoming the contradiction between the maturity of the

revolutionary conditions and the immaturity
of the proletariat.

-Trotsky (1977) *The Transitional Program*, pp. 111-114.

Bibliography.

Callinicos, A (2014) *Deciphering Capital*, London: Bookmarks.

Choonara, J (2007*) Unravelling Capitalism*, London: Bookmarks.

Cliff, T (2000) *Marxism at the Millennium*, London: Bookmarks.

Harman, C (2007) *http://isj.org.uk/therateofprofitandtheworldtoday/*

Marx, K (1974) *Capital Vol 1*, London: Lawrence & Wishart.

Marx, K (1974) *Capital Vol 3*, London: Lawrence & Wishart.   .

Mark, K (1977) *Early Writings*, Harmondsworth: Penguin Marx Library.

Trotsky (1977) *The Transitional Program for Socialist Revolution*, New York: Pathfinder Press

www.ingramcontent.com/pod-product-compliance
Lightning Source LLC
Chambersburg PA
CBHW051304250626
47155CB00009B/3424